Praise for *Ar*

'Chloe Lane is expert at taking us and mind of her character Georgie, showing us her most intimate desires with exquisitely agonising clarity.' —Claire Fuller, author of *The Memory of Animals*

'This beautifully crafted novel lights the story on fire, letting it cleanse as it burns, revealing in its wake things that cannot be erased...The smoke, humidity, and strangeness of Florida are palpable, mirroring a domestic world that threatens to smother.' —Gillian Best, author of *The Last Wave*

'This intense examination of a marriage with its rifts and sorrows had me spellbound.' —Fiona Kidman, author of *This Mortal Boy*

'Zigzags between comedy and despair...This perceptive, nuanced novel charts the murky, contingent boundaries we draw around our homes and hearts.' —Kirsten McDougall, author of *She's a Killer*

'An astute, fine-grained novel about the fires we light to sustain ourselves—and what happens when they get out of control.' —Emily Perkins, author of *The Forrests*

'*Arms & Legs* is a gritty, sexy novel that will have you aching for its characters, for the things they can and cannot say to each other.' —Sue Orr, author of *Loop Tracks*

'For all the brooding unease of the evocatively captured Southern US setting, it is the risk that we pose, sometimes unwittingly, to ourselves and those closest to us that lingers in this accomplished and absorbing novel.' —*New Zealand Listener*

'*Arms & Legs*, more than anything, gives you the feeling of having witnessed something authentic, something palpable. Though it is fiction, there is an emotional resonance, an emotional truth, to Lane's words.' —*Academy of NZ Literature*

'*Arms & Legs* has a bright intelligence and intensity. Lane is a wonderfully attentive and insightful writer. It is also at times tartly funny with an eye not just for the quiet moments in life but also the absurd.' —*NZ Herald*

'Lane's narrative is instantly compelling, as uncomfortable as it is intimate, making it impossible to look away.' —*Kete Books*

'One of [Lane's] finest skills as a writer is never turning away from the more difficult or disgusting sides of human nature.' —*Woman magazine*

'With its puzzledness and tendency for narrative swerve *Arms & Legs* reads a bit like Murakami. I was thankful for Lane's thoughtfulness and sense of quiet, particularly at the novel's surprising ending.' —*Newsroom*

'Georgie's distracted thoughts and the inconstancy of her desires are held together by [Lane's] finely and sympathetically drawn portrait of the minutiae of early parenthood.' —*Landfall Review*

'The story is this fascinating, intimate, tightly controlled and utterly compelling look at how we navigate life when it throws us wildness.' —*Nine to Noon, RNZ*

© Peter Gouge

CHLOE LANE earned her MFA in fiction at the University of Florida. She is also a graduate of the International Institute of Modern Letters at Victoria University of Wellington and the founding editor of Hue+Cry Press. Her first novel was *The Swimmers*. She lives in Gainesville, Florida.

wait till we can hang out again. Holly Beth Pratt, I am so lucky to have you. There are parts of this book that I couldn't have got right without your insight. Your love and support mean the world to me. I miss you every day.

Thank you, Padgett Powell. Thank you, David Leavitt, for your generosity, enthusiasm, and friendship. I can't wait till we can Volta coffee together again. And, Jill Ciment, though I wrote a lot of this book on the other side of the world from you, I don't think a day went by when I didn't ask myself, 'What Would Jill Do?' You have taught me so much, and you continue to teach me so much. Thank you for being an early reader of this book, and for your friendship. I miss you, and can't wait till we can again have beers together on the balcony.

Thank you, David Cauchi, for the book's cover images, and, Rose Miller, for the design.

Thank you, Craig Gamble, Kyleigh Hodgson, Tayi Tibble, and Ashleigh Young, everyone at Te Herenga Waka University Press for your enthusiasm, kindness, and patience. Thank you, Fergus Barrowman, for everything that you do. I love being a part of the Te Herenga Waka University Press family. And a very special thank you to Anna Knox, my editor. Working with you was a joy and a riot.

Thank you, Barry Hannah, for writing the story that I quote in this book, and from where the book gets its title: 'Love Too Long' from *Airships*. I read this story very early on in my writing life, and it has never left me.

Thank you, Mum, Dad, Charles, Rebecca, Fletcher, Arthur, Ivy, Henry, Lydia, Phil and Jenny for everything you do to support me and my life.

Lastly, Peter and Errol. Thank you for the love and space that allowed me to write this book. It's for you.

Acknowledgements

This book wouldn't have been possible without the support of Creative New Zealand.

I am incredibly grateful to Grimshaw & Co. and the Frank Sargeson Trust and trustees for funding my time as a Grimshaw Sargeson Fellow. A special thank you to Martin and Jenny Cole and Anna Hodge for your kindness and for making me feel so at home in the Princes Street apartment.

Thank you, Rebecca Donaldson and the Hagley College Writer in Residency Program. Thank you, Hagley Writers' Institute, Zoë Meager, Faith Oxenbridge, and to all my students. Thank you, Sarah Madison Duff at the University of Florida's Department of Ophthalmology.

Thank you to all my friends who have, over the duration of the writing of this book, supported me and allowed me a lot of *airtime*. Pip Adam, Kathryn Alley, Sarah Jane Barnett, Liv Boyle, Jill Coste, Trevor Crown, Jade Farley, Victor Florence, RL Goldberg, Sarah Gruiters, Wynne Hungerford, Biz Kechejian, Glen Lindquist, Christa Longo, Andrew McLeod, Ahby Mane, Gwen Norcliffe, Ashley Ortiz-Diaz, Victoria Palombit, Elliot Reed, Thomas Sanders, Luke Shaw, and Zina Swanson, I love you all.

Amy Brown, I am grateful for our correspondence. I can't think of this book without thinking of you and our fifteen years of friendship. I can't wait for your new book to be out in the world too. Charlie Sterchi, thank you for always sharing photos of your sandwiches with me, and for your generosity when it came to my many questions that were often only tenuously connected to the writing of this book. I miss you, and I can't

'This part, I hate it.'

'Hold on.'

It scared me, the not knowing where I was exactly. Though there was something about this feeling, of being so enveloped by smoke, that I enjoyed too. It was a bit like sticking my head underwater, which was some of the comfort I got from swimming, the dense deafening wash of that. It was also like hearing the *glub-glub* of Finn's white-noise machine running all night, which I couldn't sleep without either now. These things, in their own ways, they made me feel held and like I could handle it.

'I can't see a thing,' I said, though it was obvious and unnecessary. I think I just wanted to use my voice and to hear it out there.

Almost as soon as I spoke the wind shifted, and as quickly as the smoke had descended, it lifted away. Once again, there was the forest. The short and tall grasses, crackling and hot, the blackening trunks of the trees, the afternoon sun winking through the canopy, and the smoke, rising, rising, and rolling back on itself like a large wool sweater being shook out, to be folded and stored away for another season.

'Now I can,' I said.

I only wanted to use my voice. I needed to hear it out there.

Arms & Legs

A Novel

Chloe Lane

ANANSI
INTERNATIONAL

Published in Canada in 2024 and the USA in 2024 by House of Anansi Press Inc.
houseofanansi.com

House of Anansi Press is committed to protecting our natural environment. This book is made of material from well-managed FSC®-certified forests, recycled materials, and other controlled sources.

House of Anansi Press is a Global Certified Accessible™ (GCA by Benetech) publisher. The ebook version of this book meets stringent accessibility standards and is available to readers with print disabilities.

28 27 26 25 24   1 2 3 4 5

Library and Archives Canada Cataloguing in Publication

Title: Arms & legs : a novel / Chloe Lane.
Other titles: Arms and legs
Names: Lane, Chloe, 1982- author.
Identifiers: Canadiana (print) 20230483429 | Canadiana (ebook) 2023048347X | ISBN 9781487012038 (softcover) | ISBN 9781487012045 (EPUB)
Classification: LCC PR9639.4.L36 A76 2024 | DDC 823/.92—dc23

Cover design: Alysia Shewchuk, adapted from an original design by Rose Miller
Cover artwork: David Cauchi

House of Anansi Press is grateful for the privilege to work on and create from the Traditional Territory of many Nations, including the Anishinabeg, the Wendat, and the Haudenosaunee, as well as the Treaty Lands of the Mississaugas of the Credit.

 Canada Council for the Arts   Conseil des Arts du Canada   ONTARIO ARTS COUNCIL / CONSEIL DES ARTS DE L'ONTARIO

With the participation of the Government of Canada
Avec la participation du gouvernement du Canada | Canadä

We acknowledge for their financial support of our publishing program the Canada Council for the Arts, the Ontario Arts Council, and the Government of Canada.

Printed and bound in Canada

Peter and Errol

1.

'I can't find the pieces,' Dan said. 'The broken pieces of teeth.'

'They're not on the floor?' I said.

It was Friday afternoon and I'd just finished teaching for the week. I'd stripped down to my swimsuit and was about to get into the university pool when Dan had called to say Finn, our almost two-year-old, had tripped and fallen face-first onto the ceramic kitchen floor tiles, breaking clear both of his top front teeth.

'Not skittered into a corner?' I said.

'What if he swallowed them?' Dan said.

'If you can't find them,' I said, 'then I guess that's what happened.'

'Oh god,' Dan said. 'I'm so sorry, buddy.'

'Do you need me to come home?' I said.

The outdoor pool shimmered. I could feel the good familiar pressure of my goggles and cap tucked under the elastic of my swimsuit. I listened to Dan breathing sharply, worriedly.

I pictured him standing in the living room, his eyes fast on our boy, trying to discern if the lost shards of teeth were busy tearing holes in Finn's oesophagus and guts. I think he'd forgotten I was still on the line.

'I'll be on the next bus,' I said.

It was the first time since Finn's birth that I'd watched Dan carry the full weight of responsibility. Seeing Dan so worked up for once made me feel the opposite—calm and unconcerned. Before this incident I couldn't have guessed what a paediatric dental emergency would have looked like. This was it: a falling, a breakage, the potential for infection or long-term damage, especially if those teeth hit the floor as hard as Dan said and as a result of the impact were pushed too far up inside their soft gums, drilling in via their own roots.

As we passed through the automatic doors of the clinic, which was hidden away in a satellite wing of the University Hospital, we were hit with a wave of air-conditioning, bright lights, and eerie calm sprinkled with a distant swelling of Tom Petty's 'Free Fallin''. Finn had been doing admirably, curious only to see where we were going together in the car at this unexpected hour. Now he became fearful. He cried throughout the examination, he shook and sobbed during the x-ray. That was the one shred in my calm: Finn in my lap, mouth full of plastic claws and film, the two of us pressed neck to knees by the weight of a heavy lead vest. As Finn howled through all that equipment, I felt myself wanting to cry too, my breathing growing jagged and shallow to match my boy's.

The dentist was in his early thirties, a Florida cowboy, thin and tanned. After he explained about watching for bubbles on Finn's gums—painful white specks that were a sign something was wrong—he laid out options for cosmetic repair.

'Yeah, I don't think so,' Dan said, interrupting him.

Though the dentist and his graduate assistant remained professional throughout, the air between them was uncomfortably thick with sex. The temperature of Dan's manner made me think he sensed it too.

'I want you to know it's an option,' the dentist said.

By this point, Finn's unhappiness had simmered down to silent tears. I couldn't help but imagine him with a mouth full of crowns, teeth big and smooth, the gaps between each sharp kernel filled in, a boy for a pageant. Though it had been almost six years since Dan and I had moved to Florida from New Zealand, I wanted to flirt with the idea for a moment simply because it seemed a very American way to respond to such a minor injury. Even after all this time, maybe especially after all this time, I was still interested in remaking myself in this way, as an American.

'No, no options,' Dan said.

'We can do it in kids as young as this,' the dentist said. 'No problem at all.'

'I'm sure you can,' Dan said, 'but we gotta get our boy home.'

Dan and Finn were already halfway out the door when the dentist calmly folded his arms against his chest, leaned back in his swivel chair, the lanky prince of North Central Florida paediatric dentistry, and gave me a look that said, *Next time.*

How did I respond? It matters not because the dentist would end up having any place in this story, but because as I returned the dentist's look, I felt myself trying to communicate something wrong. Not for the first time, but this time Dan was right there. Finn falling, Dan shook up and shouldering it all, had resulted in an unexpected softening of my load that momentarily made me feel unworried, thrillingly careless. This was how I responded: *Yes.*

2.

Over breakfast the next morning Dan offered to get a vasectomy. Neither of us wanted more children and, in the past when this topic had been half-heartedly raised, I'd expressed support for Dan's willingness to take charge and the freedom it implied. This time it bothered me. It felt like it came out of nowhere. I think it was the result of an internal panic Dan had been stewing on since Finn's fall, about parenthood and responsibility. His role. The breaking of Finn's teeth had made Dan freshly vulnerable and uncertain, maybe got him picturing the breaking of other things. I didn't want to have children with any other man, definitely not Jason, nor did I want Dan to have children with anyone else, but for some reason at this time the loose strings of that possibility were comforting to me in a way that the image of Dan, Finn and me sealed into a circle wasn't.

So, when Dan brought up the vasectomy, I said, 'That's okay, you don't have to do that.'

Dan responded by quietly folding and sealing himself up like an envelope.

I suggested we go for a family walk.

An hour later I found myself standing in the flat heat of the prairie with Finn awkwardly hanging from me in a front-pack he'd long outgrown, looking at a bald eagle. The binoculars were heavy and I'd been regretting bringing them. Not now. My first bald eagle. It was sitting high in a pine tree preening its breast.

'It sounds like a squirrel,' Dan said, indignant beside me.

I also thought the eagle would have a bigger voice. That high shriek, more like the complaint of a nothing seagull, was not how I had imagined the majestic call of America's bird.

'I'm looking right at it,' I said. 'Wow. There you are.'

I understood the sounds coming from Finn to mean this: 'Wow.'

'Wow,' I said, 'that's right.'

'Can I see?' Dan said. He reached for the binoculars. I handed them over.

The first time we visited the prairie, our first winter in Florida, I'd been stunned by the tall, dry and seedy grasses, so many shades of yellow and brown, some freckled with flowers, the sky hard and blue and cloudless, and except for the birds, the only signs of animal life droppings left by wild horses, shallow and cracked gator tracks. In summer, it was a completely different scene. Much of the track was flooded and everything was lush and wet—the Florida I'd always imagined. Back in New Zealand there were the pōhutukawa in December—every year it was a pleasure to see the first crimson blooms pop—otherwise, when I thought of the landscape of my homeland it was always the same, no matter what the season, though that couldn't be right.

Finn began aggressively arching against me, while expelling a river of indecipherable sounds. I could make out one word: 'Stuck.'

That day the prairie was somewhere in the space between winter and spring. There was a rustling in the surrounds, a feeling that things were ready to burst forth, but not yet, not quite.

'I know you want to get out,' I said, 'but you can't. It's not safe.'

Again, Finn with his rush of noise—this time the wave cresting with: 'Out.'

'Would you like some water?' I said. I clicked my fingers at Dan. 'Bottle, please.'

Dan was standing motionless a few feet away, silently looking through the binoculars. When we first met, I was initially attracted to his tallness. He was six-three and skinny, with a presence that was close to apologetic—the result of spending his life trying to fold himself down to the level of his peers. Then he'd smiled for me and his snaggletooth had sealed it.

'I can't see it,' he said. 'It must've moved. You sure it was an eagle?'

'I'm sure,' I said. 'Try taking off your glasses.'

Dan did as I suggested and hooked his glasses into the neck of his T-shirt. He removed his cap too. His hair had been down his back when we met, but since we'd moved to Florida he'd kept it short and floppy in a manner that betrayed his Englishness and was also not that dissimilar to the cut I regularly gave Finn—who had inherited his dad's thick dark and fast-growing hair—in our kitchen with the blunt craft scissors.

'These binoculars are weird,' Dan said.

'Can you pass the bottle?' I said.

'They're hurting my eyes,' Dan said. 'Now it's all abstract.'

'Come on with the bottle,' I said.

'Wait, yes,' Dan said. He unzipped the backpack he was carrying and without looking at me he handed over Finn's water bottle.

Dan was naturally lowkey, a people-pleaser. If I ever irritated him he almost never showed it. I wasn't this way, but from the start of our relationship I'd taken his lead and learned to be less bothered by the little things, though that wasn't the mode between us that morning.

Dan returned to the binoculars. 'Just, why can't I see it?'

'It's probably gone,' I said. 'Why don't you give them back to me? You can carry Finn for a bit.' I lowered my mouth to Finn's ear. 'Can I take your bottle, sweetie?'

Once Finn was secured on Dan's front, I strolled off down the path on my own. The eagle had been sitting on the branch of a Florida pine in a wooded area at the south-eastern corner of the prairie and I went in that direction. I'd been carrying around an outdated map of documented nests in our county for nearly three years, thinking that, if there was an eagle nearby, I might at least be looking in the right direction. Just as I'd imagined the eagle's call as powerful and haunting, I'd similarly pictured this impressive bird nesting in only the most monumental of settings—definitely not the bare branch of a ratty pine in North Central Florida.

The first time I saw a kiwi, I was standing as close to the exhibit barrier in the zoo's dark Kiwi House as was practicable, and as my eyes adjusted, I saw a shadow shift, a slender beak, then the body of the bird as it emerged from behind a log. It

13

was both smaller and more astounding than I'd been prepared for—that very round and fluffy body, beak thin and long like my nana's crochet needles. I was next to two of my classmates and I could feel them vibrating with excitement too.

The bald eagle—it was a giant—had moved to a branch of a different tree. I didn't know how Dan could have missed it. I wondered briefly if it was only an apparition, a high-pitched creature conjured from the cloudy vault of my exhausted mind. I blinked and the eagle called out again.

'Was that it?' Dan asked. He and Finn were standing directly behind me. Dan had put his glasses and cap back on.

'I think it was,' I said.

'Can you see it?'

'No,' I lied. 'I can't.'

It was partially the thought of having to deal with Dan and the binoculars again, sensing how easily that might boil over, but that wasn't all. I also suddenly wanted to keep the eagle for myself.

'I want to look again,' Dan said.

The eagle had returned to preening its broad, dark breast. I thought about how it would feel to push my fingers down through its coarse outer feathers, and wriggle my fingertips in till they reached the soft down beneath. The bird looked up then, its serious yellow eyes wide. I felt it looking directly at me. It cocked its head and said, 'I see you.' A lump formed in the back of my throat. I kept the binoculars to my eyes, as if they were plugs keeping something in.

'Too late,' I said. 'It's gone.'

'I didn't see it go,' Dan said.

'Believe me or don't believe me,' I said.

When I finally lowered the binoculars, Dan and Finn, the

14

large and small figures of them bound together, had already begun walking back up the track and away.

The city in which we lived—and that was what it called itself: *The City of*—was a university town. Our neighbourhood was situated a mile from campus in the city's historic district, which meant a lot of two-storey wooden houses, some that had been lovingly restored and were mostly lived in by professors and their families, and some that were rentals occupied by grad students or working folks and that looked as if they were begging for a sinkhole to swallow them down. On the drive home from the prairie our late-Nineties-model Honda came to a not wholly unexpected spluttering stop on the side of the road. We were still several miles from our neighbourhood in a part of the wider town that reminded me of where I'd grown up in New Zealand, where the only signs of municipality were a lone bus stop, recently repainted road markers, and letterboxes pinpointing a scattering of driveways.

'What's going on?' I said.

Dan was sitting silently behind the wheel.

'I said, what's going on?' My tone was immediately accusatory.

'That's not good,' Dan said. He turned the key twice more. Each time, nothing.

'What does that mean?' I said.

Dan dropped his hands into his lap.

'I'll call Triple-A,' I said.

'Go for it,' Dan said, 'but it'll be a waste of time.'

'Why?' I said, though I knew why. Our Triple-A membership had been one of the expenses I'd suggested we cut once Finn arrived.

Dan was slumped and staring out the front windscreen, the soft swell of a middle-aged chin visible, a single bold nose hair peeping out. It had been a while since we'd had sex, or even moved towards each other in that way. Dan was an enormously quiet man. By the time we met, both of us in our later twenties, this was what I'd wanted. I was ready for a relationship where I could just exist, kindly and calmly, and in no time at all we had moved in together, got married, and were packing our bags for Florida. None of these things had felt big because more than that they had felt right, and for several years we'd been happy. Then Finn had arrived, and Dan had proceeded to slide away from me. I'd been prepared for this, and already I thought I could feel him returning, but his drift—I was certain that was why I'd slid towards and then finally, as of last night, fucked Jason.

I looked out the front windscreen too. It was filthy. I couldn't remember when either of us had last cleaned it. It might have been after we returned from our road trip to West Texas, the occasion we had to bump up our Triple-A membership to the premium level. That was several springs ago, so a lifetime ago.

Finn was starting to grumble.

'You're okay,' I said. 'We'll be home soon.'

'Hmm,' Dan said.

'What about one of these places?' I said, nodding at the few letterboxes visible on the road ahead of us. 'Maybe someone could give us a jump-start?'

I could see Dan thinking this through. Asking a stranger for help, walking home, getting an Uber, calling a friend for assistance—which option would be the least expensive, which was the favour that would annoy the least number of people, the favour he might not have to return unexpectedly down the line when he didn't want to? Dan wasn't ungenerous, he just liked to do things on his own time, and he didn't like to be in debt.

'Yeah, all right,' he said.

I didn't bother with the pack, instead carrying Finn on my hip. No one was home at the first two houses. As we ventured down the longer, sandy driveway of the third address, where an enormous rambling bungalow rose in the distance, we came upon a dead squirrel. It was lying on the verge on its back with its arms stretched above its head, not so different to how Finn liked to sleep. It would prove to be a bad omen, though right then we had some fun with it.

'How do you think it died?' I said. 'Do you think it fell from a tree? Got hit by a car? Was it sick? Did it fall while trying to mate?'

'Probably sick,' Dan said.

'It didn't look sick.'

'How do you know what squirrel cancer looks like?'

'I've seen a squirrel with bald patches all over its body and tangled up in Spanish moss. Like the one I fished out of that bucket of water.'

'That *you* fished out?'

'Maybe it died of old age,' I said. 'Or a heart attack.'

'It looked fat.'

'It probably ate too many nuts,' I said.

'Too many honey-roasted nuts.'

I snorted at Dan's joke. I glanced in his direction and saw he was smiling too. The silly back-and-forth about the squirrel filled me up. I remember thinking in that moment that it had been days since I'd seen Dan smile properly. The fresh warmth between us was proof that my suggesting we go for a walk together had been correct.

When we reached the bungalow, we were met by a sleek young pit bull. The dog was straining on his rope so it was taut, and barking and furiously wagging his tail. I could tell he was still young by his paws—those feet, he was still growing into them. Before we could take a single step back, the screen door of the porch opened and a man in his sixties wearing belted cargo shorts and a short-sleeved button-down shirt appeared at the top of the steps.

'He comes from royalty,' he called out, 'but don't mind him, he won't do a thing to you.'

'Our car's broken down,' I said, over Finn's head, which was resting heavy on my shoulder.

The man, who introduced himself as Gray 'with an A', whistled to his dog. The dog, who he introduced as Ernie Boy, immediately stopped straining on his rope and trotted across to Gray and sat down at the foot of the steps.

Dan chimed in now. 'Wondering if we could get a jump-start?'

'It's the battery?' Gray asked.

'Honestly,' Dan said, 'I don't know.' He sounded crushed.

'Hold on then.' Gray disappeared inside the house for a minute. When he returned he was wearing a pair of scuffed leather loafers and a blue trucker cap. He untied Ernie Boy, attached a short lead to his collar, and the two of them joined Dan, Finn and me in the middle of the yard.

'Your accents,' Gray said. 'You're from somewhere in the South Pacific. I wouldn't like to venture a guess, wouldn't want to cause offence.'

'New Zealand,' I said.

Gray nodded, as if he knew this already. 'I have a cousin who moved down your way in the Nineteen Eighties. All I know of New Zealand is what this cousin once wrote me about the state of the wind there. That being that there's a lot of it and it's big.'

'Really?' I said. 'Cool.'

This was my standard response whenever someone told me they knew someone who either lived in New Zealand or had once visited there, followed by this kind of anecdote. The questions that usually came next—the ones about what we were doing in Florida, to which I would reply, I was studying at first, yes at the university, a Masters in Education, yes I'd finished, yes I was adjunct teaching, technical writing to engineering students mostly, yes Dan worked too, no he was also a Kiwi, yes we had green cards now, from the lottery, yes we were lucky, yes we loved it here, yes even with things as they currently were, no really this was our home—Gray didn't ask.

'Ernie Boy and I will follow in the truck,' was all Gray said. 'Lead the way.'

It wasn't the battery, but a bolt-like part that needed replacing, and which Gray miraculously had a spare of. 'And why did I have this?' Gray said to himself while inspecting his work. 'No clue, no clue, no clue.' He shook his head with pleasure.

'How much do we owe you?' Dan asked.

Gray looked up, incredulous. While maintaining eye-contact with Dan, he reached into his back pocket and withdrew his wallet. He removed a black and white photograph, which he held out for me to see.

'That's his great-granddaddy,' he said.

The photograph was of a pit bull that looked identical to Ernie Boy but with the muscular silhouette of a ten-wheeler.

'What a dog,' I said.

'That's fighting dog royalty right there,' Gray said.

While Gray had been making the repairs, Ernie Boy had remained sitting in the passenger seat of the truck. For the most part, he had been sitting quietly. Now he started to bark.

'Quit it,' Gray said, over his shoulder.

'He wants to get out,' I said. 'Stretch his legs.'

'Two hundred and thirty-five pounds,' Gray said.

I could tell by the look on Dan's face that he thought this was what Gray wanted in payment for the repair.

When neither of us immediately responded, Gray added, 'That's a pit bull's bite strength. Not the most powerful of the Canidae lot, but still something.'

'Did you hear that, Finn?' I said.

'I'll demonstrate for you,' Gray said.

'Hmm,' Dan said.

This 'hmm' thing was a recent addition to Dan's purse of noises. I didn't know if he even realised he was doing it. I could sense that he was getting antsy, but I didn't see how we couldn't follow Gray back down his driveway. Anyway, I wanted to follow him.

A thick rope had been tied to a branch of a live oak in the corner of Gray's yard, about forty feet up. At the bottom of the rope was a large knot dangling some five feet from the ground. Gray handed Dan the knot and told him to swing it. Dan pulled it back a few paces and let it drop, and Ernie Boy took a running leap and latched on to the knot with his strong jaw.

Gray stood back and crossed his arms against his chest like a proud dad.

'That doesn't hurt him?' Dan asked.

Gray shook his head.

'You see that, Finn?' I said.

20

I understood one word from Finn: 'Dog.' Once he'd got it out, he made a noise, a snort that somewhat resembled a woof. It came out of his nose, quietly, his mouth open enough to reveal his broken teeth.

'That's right,' I said. 'A dog. Woof-woof.'

Finn made the sound again but louder and more confidently this time.

Gray wasn't watching us, but when I glanced in his direction, I could see him smiling in a way that suggested he was listening. Finn hadn't met any of his grandparents. Dan's mother had died just over a year after Dan and I got together. My parents and Dan's dad were all in New Zealand, and no one had come to visit since Finn's birth, and we hadn't been back since before I was pregnant—the trip that coincided with our green card interviews. I felt sad about this, though maybe not sad enough.

As we watched Ernie Boy swinging back and forth, his eyes darting to keep Gray in his line of vision, I looked casually around Gray's property. I saw a sliver of swimming pool poking out from behind the house. A pair of swimming trunks and a long-sleeved swim shirt were drying draped over the back of a lounger. Propped up beside it was a water-walking belt.

'Is your pool heated?' I asked.

'Only to eighty,' Gray said, almost as if he couldn't believe I hadn't already known this. 'I turn on the heat as soon as the nights dip below seventy. Soon it'll be warm enough to not have to bother with that.'

Dan was standing close to me but we weren't touching. Finn's bare legs were swinging where they hung either side of my hip. Dan reached out and took one of Finn's soft feet in his hand. These days, this was the closest Dan and I got to holding hands. Until Jason had pressed his arm against my arm for the first time last month, the two of us leaning against the issuing desk on the children's floor of the library, it was an absence I'd started to get used to—it was an absence that had taken up space. Though in this moment I felt it for what it was—just air.

Now Dan hoisted Finn from my arms. The weight and warmth of him had been keeping me grounded. I started thinking about Jason. It wasn't the right place to do it, but as the four of us stood in silence and watched Ernie Boy swing, I allowed myself a moment back there.

It had taken Jason no time to open the door last evening. Framed by the dim light in his hallway, he'd greeted me barefoot in black cut-offs and a black T-shirt. The way Jason had presented himself to me is, I knew, how Dan would present himself if he were opening the door to another woman. It wasn't that they looked startlingly alike, Dan tall and thin, Jason shorter and denser, but from the outside they weren't that different either. They were a similar kind of man. Jason though. Before he'd spoken, he'd reached up and absently raked his fingers across the greying buzzcut that either gave him a sweet, boyish air or the bluntness of a petty criminal. Then he'd said, with a nothing friendliness, as if I'd arrived to give him a clarinet lesson or repair his fridge, 'Hey, Georgie.' He'd lived in Alabama till after he'd graduated college and his voice killed me. *Hey, Georgie.* My name in his mouth. As soon as we heard the door click and were alone, it was as if something was loosened, a ribbon pulled free of itself, and we stepped in, no time to think before I could feel the heat of him and his lips against mine, his tongue teasing my mouth open. He tasted like nothing. He smelled a bit of toothpaste—a lone peak above the plain of his own scent. I couldn't lean in far enough. I felt him grunt, a little satisfied click in the back of his throat, which I mirrored.

These memories swarmed up over me like an organisation of fire ants, sharp and diverting. It was a different kind of grounding. I didn't yet feel any guilt. This beginning sequence, Jason and me both still clothed, thinking about it made me feel extraordinary. It was as far as I got into remembering that evening, before I clicked back to where I was—Gray's yard, the sun warming the top of my head, the scrappy grass beneath my feet curling up around my ankles, the sudden red swoop of a cardinal emerging from a nearby shrub, Dan anxiously tapping the fingers of his free hand against his leg.

'What's that parked beside the pool?' Dan said.

'That's my fire engine,' Gray said. 'We'll start burning as soon as we get a good frost.'

'Burning?' Dan said.

'Correct,' Gray said.

The two men continued talking. I departed again. I could sense the weight and curve of Jason's body pressed against mine, my back pressed hard against the hallway wall. I was trying to recreate the feeling of being in that moment, the rapid pace of my pulse, the radiating ache of my pelvis, my brain turned to cushion stuffing. What came after was a different thing. This, the bridge to what came after, felt like everything and where all the answers lay.

As Dan, Finn and I were walking back up Gray's driveway to our car, which was still parked on the side of the road, I thought about what Dan and Gray had been discussing.

'Where do these prescribed burns take place?' I asked.

'All over, I guess,' Dan said, absently. He appeared lost in his own thoughts now.

23

'All over where?'

Dan gestured around him with a sweep of his arm, taking in the trees, shrubs and grasses that surrounded us on all sides, cut through only by this long sandy driveway.

The summer I was five, I learned to swim in my primary school pool. My older brother Gerard had shown me how to grip the side of the pool and kick furiously, how to float on my back like a felled log, how to dive to the bottom of the deep end to retrieve his dropped goggles. This was the same summer the pine forest burned.

The fire was started by a group of teenagers smoking amongst the dry pine needles. Our house sat on top of a cliff that overlooked the township, the forest an amphitheatre surrounding the town and the beach. I would come to mark a loose time by the forest's long seasons of growth, felling, replanting and growth. That summer, though, we stood on our front lawn and watched it all go up.

The local volunteer firefighters were at the front of the attack for the first terrifying day till they were joined by professionals from the city. When it looked as if the fire would never be contained—it had spread in mottled patches of heat—the rain rolled in. Storms were rare in those dry January days, and the brief but unexpectedly heavy rainfall was enough to slow down the progress of the fire and for the folks battling it to get it under control. Every adult who came to our house in the days following exhaled in relief and in the same breath said, 'We're bloody blessed, bloody blessed,' or, 'Someone was watching out for us, eh?' None of these people were God-fearing, unless you meant the gods of the sea, surfing and boozy barbecues. When it was over and the clouds and smoke lifted, there was the hillside, a puzzle of bare and black earth with areas of trees still untouched. The landscape looked horribly deformed, sick.

I've often wondered about the teenagers who started the fire and how they must have felt when they saw the first line of smoke rising from the dry, needly undergrowth. Did they try and stamp it out with their jandals? Did someone remove their sweater and try and beat back the fresh licks of flame? Did they curse and point fingers—whose cigarette butt was at fault? And how long before they realised they could do nothing but run? As they watched the fire grow and spread over the hours that followed, what hell they must have endured.

During this time, every night after I'd put on my pyjamas and brushed my teeth, I packed my best clothes and toys into two plastic shopping bags and my school backpack, and arranged them in a line by the front door. If we had to leave in a hurry, I was ready. When I eventually slept, I dreamed of scorched earth, waking at a chilled hour prickled with sweat, and unable to find a way back to sleep. This continued well after the fire had been extinguished. I turned tired and pathetic. I stopped eating. It probably never occurred to our family doctor to prescribe me anything more than letting me eat whatever and whenever, and to otherwise keep me occupied.

After a while, the nightmares did fade, and I eventually stopped packing my bags at night, but my big uneasiness about fire never completely went away. Until I was well into my twenties, I refused to cook on a gas stove, barbecues made me nervous, and fireworks were a straight-up no-go. The first time I saw Dan slide his lighter into his jeans pocket, I thought: Great, now I can never love this man.

Finn had wanted to walk up the driveway on his own. He put a few feet between us before he came to a halt, his attention caught by something in the ground.

'I hope that's not a snake,' I said, though I could clearly see there was no snake there. 'Or another dead squirrel.'

I heard Dan inhale sharply. This was how he gathered his thoughts, as if he had to physically suck them up from around him to inside him. It was in his nature to take this time before speaking his mind, which I sensed he was gearing up to do now. I'd found this frustrating when we first started dating, but I'd since gotten used to it, and I let him have it. Finn turned and faced us, rabidly waving a leaf.

We'd arrived at the car when Dan finally spoke.

'Are you even attracted to me anymore?' he said.

On reflection, the line that connected my outward ambivalence about Dan getting a vasectomy to this question was clear. But it was the last thing in the world I expected Dan to ask me. It was true there hadn't been a lot of sex since Finn's arrival. And each time when we were done and I'd caught my breath and come back down from where I'd been floating up near the ceiling, for Dan had never not been a good lay, that wasn't our problem, I'd said to him, 'Did that feel weird? Do I feel weird? Different?' Though he'd always assured me that it didn't feel weird, that I felt good and the same, still I lay in the dark for hours afterwards feeling desolate and exposed. Dan had been on the front lines for Finn's birth. Though I'd had no issue with it at the time, and that wasn't even what I was thinking about in the dark, I wondered if that was a contributing factor for the . . . lull? For, what had Dan seen? He remained *vague*. There's nothing mysterious about the human body really, it is what it is and it does what it does, except no one had prepared me for how exposed and also the opposite of that—so turned in on myself—I would continue to feel once it was all over with, even after all this time, the alchemy of those two states so out of whack.

I still hadn't answered Dan's question. I'd paused too long.

I heard a screech then. It wasn't a Finn noise—he was right there seriously inspecting something new by the back wheel of our car. It gave me a fright though. Another kid was yelling from a house across the road, happily or unhappily, I don't know, it wasn't always easy to make that distinction.

'Yes,' I said to Dan, 'I'm still attracted to you.'

Before either of us could say anything else, I turned my back to Dan and bent down to see what Finn was grabbing at. This time it was the dried and flattened remains of a tailless lizard.

I thought I knew all about the loneliness and sadness of new motherhood. I also thought I'd felt it starting to lift. At some point, though, what had begun as a side-effect of sleeplessness and the crushing weight of carrying the entire domestic load had taken root in the heart of my marriage as a deep and blooming dissatisfaction. As Finn's accident had shaken something up in Dan, Jason had shaken something different up in me. In the past months I'd become convinced I'd been sleepwalking through my life. I'd started to picture myself as the transparent casing of a snakeskin, shed and twitching in the feeble Florida breeze. There was nothing to me and I was sick of it, feeling that way. I'd started to believe that if I gathered up enough moments where my heart raced in a good way and stuffed them down inside me, things that were mine alone, like the bald eagle, like Jason, then I would gain a budding fullness and opacity and I would feel better.

I couldn't yet know the significance of this day, which was

my chance meeting of Gray, Dan's spying of the fire engine, and the slowly developing storm of an idea that would lead me into the forest on my first burn. It was the bald eagle I thought of as we drove home. Both how it had made me feel, and how I'd kept it from Dan. It was a small thing, the tiniest of lies, and yet there was something in the lie's innocuous nature that made it feel more damaging than the other bigger lie of the last two days. I couldn't say why exactly I'd done it, not letting Dan see that bird too. I feared that it was in this not knowing, and the fuzzy space that was expanding between Dan and me, that the not-so-minor illness of our marriage was incubating.

3.

Two Thursdays later I was in the forest with Gray and a group of other experienced prescribed burners—Ed, Gerry and Fran, an older couple Doug and Dottie, and two rangers who were both named Darby.

'This is Darby,' Gray said, pointing to one of them, and pointing to the other, 'That's also Darby.'

'You don't need to worry about that,' the first Darby said.

Dry grasses and trees surrounded me on all sides. The earth was hard beneath my feet. Faint animal tracks cut a line between some pines. The smell of smoke wafted in our direction from across the forest where another burn was underway. I'd failed to pack my water bottle. One recent afternoon I'd taken a break from grading papers to buy a rooibos tea from the campus Starbucks nearest my shared office. When the barista had asked if I would like it iced, inexplicably I'd said yes. In the smoky heat of the forest I wished I were drinking that beverage. It had been like slurping rainwater directly from the mucky bark of a

29

tree. None of the plants around me looked like they would be a good source of hydration if I got stranded out there with Gray and his friends.

The first time I spoke with Gray after the morning our car broke down, he'd told me his team did most of their burning in April. So, on Tuesday when I'd lunched with him for the second time in his campus office and he'd said they would be burning today, I'd been surprised.

Now I looked down at the gloves Gray had lent me. They were too large, like two baseball mitts. I'd assumed I would only be a silent observer of these events. Instead, I was lining up to get a drip torch.

'Have you ever handled a torch?' Ed asked.

Ed and Gray were identically dressed in belted shorts and short-sleeved button-down shirts, though on this occasion the loafers I'd become accustomed to seeing on Gray had been substituted for leather boots. The two of them were also wearing gloves and hard hats.

'No,' I said to Ed, 'I've never had an occasion to handle a drip torch.'

I was wearing a hard hat too.

'It's a piece of cake,' Ed said.

Gray nodded.

'Easy-peasy,' Gerry piped in.

Gerry looked like a botanist. He was a tiny man, bespectacled, and dressed in cargo pants with zip-off legs, large hiking boots, and over some kind of high-tech long-sleeved shirt he was wearing a canvas vest drunk with pockets.

'Should I be wearing fire-proof clothing?' I asked on spying Gerry's top.

Gray waved off my question. 'Ed'll light you up further

down the track.'

'Do I hold it like this?' I said. I could hear the nervousness in my voice.

'Down the ways a bit,' Gerry said.

'That's what I said,' Gray said.

I'd had no problem tracking Gray down. I'd been seeking a distraction from Jason, who in the days since that first Friday I'd seen three more times, the initial thrill of us already unravelling in a bad way into something else. I also thought that witnessing a prescribed burn was simply something I would like to do.

Gray was a professor in a special branch of the university's Food and Agricultural Services wing, a scholar of plant pathology, I'd learned as we had been leaving his house, and I'd sought him out the following week. His office was in a secluded, almost rural, corner of the sprawling campus, and when he discovered I was interested in prescribed burns he had invited me to join one. I hadn't told Dan about the burn, though he knew I'd met up with Gray. He thought I was on campus that afternoon finishing up my weekly office hours, not in the middle of the forest listening to Gray and Gerry discussing a new citrus greening study from a rival university.

'When it first arrived,' Gray said, 'we were concerned, but not panicked. Our trees, we thought they'd be all right. We thought they were tough.'

'I know that,' Gerry said. 'You forget that I was there.'

'I do not forget,' Gray said, his voice still ripe with the memory of his folly.

'This new study, I gotta say,' Gerry said. 'I'm not on board, Gray, I'm not.'

Gray had spoken passionately to me on the topics of snake conservation, hurricane preparedness, the flooding in the

31

aftermath of Irma, Florida's aquifers, the heyday of Texas dog-fighting, canine humour, the migratory patterns of the blue-gray gnatcatcher, and at the end of our first lunch he'd recited in detail the recipe for his version of squirrel gumbo. Citrus greening was his area of expertise, though, and he had outlined the basics. This was how I understood some of what he and Gerry were saying.

'It turned out this disease was one of the biggies,' Gray said now. 'You can go ahead, play your gene-editing games and create a tree that can't be infected with the disease. Most growers, though, they don't have the resources to chop down sick trees and plant new ones.'

'No,' I said, 'I imagine not.'

'We're fighting them from the inside out. From the phloem out,' Gerry said.

I felt Fran nudge my elbow. She was wearing very dark sunglasses, her cured complexion that of someone who had spent their entire life in the Florida outdoors.

'Girl,' she said, 'keep the torch upright.'

Only on arriving at the burn site, after using Gray's written directions to navigate the predominantly unmarked roads, had I registered that we weren't on a small backyard burn. I was pretty sure we were in the State Park, though it was a part of the prairie and forest that I'd never seen, accessible via a long, unsealed road pocked with gopher holes. From what I could gather, Doug and Dottie were veterans of the prescribed burn scene. They had arrived in a truck with a quad bike on the back. That was how they would be getting around. The rest of us were on foot. We were working in teams of three. One of the Darbys, Doug and Dottie disappeared down a track—Darby walking, Doug driving, Dottie sitting ladylike on the back

32

of the bike. The other Darby was with Gray and Gerry. Ed, Fran and I were working together. The plot we were burning stretched from where we were standing, back over toward a wide swampy area near the highway. I was still thinking about how thirsty I was, and about being responsible for my own drip torch. I looked down at my monstrous hands and saw myself tripping and falling and setting the whole forest alight.

Gray's fire engine was parked nearby. At his house it had looked so squat and zippy, like a child's drawing of a fire engine come to life. Out here it had a threatening aura, one that made me admit to myself for the first time how terribly wrong things could go.

'You're going to be fine,' Gray said, as if reading my mind. As he left, he stopped and touched his gloved hand to Fran's back, low enough and long enough for me to understand that they were more than just burn pals.

'Let's get movin',' Ed said.

Fran walked slowly with a deliberate swing of her bony hips. She sauntered off down a different cleared path, a drip torch in one hand and a large metal spade in the other.

'We're going to start in the far corner,' Ed said. 'As soon as Doug and Dot give us the signal.' He was carrying a rake and wearing a backpack full of supplies.

'How long you think we'll be out here?' I said.

'Hard to say,' Ed said.

It had been impossible to get a time frame out of Gray. Finn was meant to be with his babysitter for only another two hours. Driving out here and getting everyone set up had taken longer than I had anticipated. I was doubtful we would be done in time, but I was also anxious about doing a good job, so I held my drip torch as level as I could and followed Ed into the trees.

'It's three parts diesel to one part gasoline,' Ed said.

I nodded as if I understood what this meant.

'The gasoline ignites it,' he said. 'The diesel fuel, well that gives it longevity. It's gonna stick to whatever it drops on and burn, burn, burn.'

My father once demonstrated for me what happens when you mix fire and petrol. I was maybe eight years old. I watched from my bedroom window as he poured a large puddle of lawnmower fuel on our gravel driveway, stepped back and lit a match, turned briefly in my direction and said, 'Watch carefully, daughter,' as he flicked the match into the puddle.

I flinched when Ed lit my drip torch.

The weight of the fuel in the canister, the feel of it sloshing around in there, alarmed me. All I had to do was tip the torch like a teapot, and out came flaming pebble-sized balls of fuel. I felt clumsy with my gloves though. It didn't feel safe. Just the afternoon before, while Finn napped, I'd watched YouTube videos about prescribed burns. In one clip, a man spoke directly to the camera about appropriate safety gear with the reluctance of someone making a ransom video. Once he had said his bit, he looked offscreen, as if towards his captors, and said, 'This place, it's dying to burn.' I thought about this again now, and realised how much I didn't want to be out there. As soon as I was holding that fire in my hands, I didn't want it. I wanted to leave so much.

'They're designed to put fire on the ground safely,' Fran said, nodding at my torch.

'It's still fire,' I said. I could hear the strain in my voice.

'You ain't wrong there,' Ed said.

'Does the fire ever climb back up the spout?' I said.

Ed looked at me.

34

'Explosions?' I said, weakly.

'It can do that,' Ed said.

I looked down at the canister in my hands and pictured this happening, a fireball so forceful it took off both my arms. The explosion of this imagining created a different kind of explosion in my brain and then my heart and I suddenly, unexpectedly found myself missing Dan. I wanted him to be there with me. I wanted to see him and to know he could see me.

When my father had lit that puddle of lawnmower fuel in my childhood driveway, it had gone *whoosh* with such a violence that I fell backwards off the bed I'd been sitting on and cracked my head on the wooden floor. There had been blood. I didn't want to be out there with Ed and Fran, holding a drip torch, pretending I was someone I wasn't. Already I had a bad feeling I was on the wrong track. I couldn't leave though—I was in it. More than anything else I didn't want to appear irresponsible or to look stupid, and so I stayed.

Fran and Ed weren't using torches right away. Instead, they followed behind me—Ed with a rake, Fran with a spade— pulling leaves and twigs here and there, helping to keep things moving in the right direction. It was my job to keep dripping and lighting the fire as they said. I got the hang of it, the fire, the heat, the weight, the anxiety of it, too, settling around my shoulders like a coarse wool shawl. After we'd been at it for a while, and the fire had started to stretch into the dry undergrowth surrounding the pines and crackle with a satisfying ferocity, the wind shifted a degree, and the smoke, wow, the smoke. I don't know why I hadn't thought about there being smoke, not in a practical sense.

'Wind's shifting a bit,' Ed said, 'but it's gonna be all right.'

'You okay?' Fran called out to me.

I was trying not to cough. No one else was coughing. I was trying not to rub my eyes.

'Masks, glasses help,' Fran said.

'We're nearly done,' Ed said.

It took us another half an hour to get our section burning to Ed's satisfaction. By the time we stopped for chicken salad sandwiches, care of Dottie, I was feeling very dehydrated and a whole new kind of exhausted. While Ed was checking in with the others on the hand-held radio, Fran took some time to explain to me that this was a dormant season burn—the second for this area, which would be ready for a 'growing burn' next season. As she spoke, she looked not at me but over my shoulder, her weight rested on her spade, her sandwich held in front of her with the kind of limp-wristed casualness you might use for a cigarette.

'Bit of an oxymoron?' I said. *'Growing burn.'*

Fran looked at me then. She said nothing.

'We're lucky,' Ed said, joining us again, 'the wind's doing it good.' He whistled in imitation of the light breeze that had helped direct the fire.

'How do you know the wind won't change suddenly?' I said.

'It won't,' Ed said. 'It's doin' it, everyone's good.'

'Faith,' Fran said.

'What happens to the animals?' I said.

'That's why we burn in plots,' Ed said. 'So they have somewhere to run to, some safety between the fires.'

I imagined the patches of land that were free of fire, like where Ed, Fran and I were currently standing, filled with deer, raccoons, armadillos, snakes, birds, lizards, frogs, insects, all the animals lined up as if they were waiting to board a bus.

'Though I guess the birds can fly away,' I said. 'Unless

they're very young birds.'

'That's why we burn this time of the year,' Fran said, maybe seeing the look on my face as I thought about all the baby birds feeling the heat of the fire draw near and being unable to do anything about it. 'Less chance of that. A lot of animals burrow underground too.'

I looked at my phone. I had three missed calls from Amber, Finn's babysitter. She might have called Dan by now too. I wanted someone to tell me I could go home. Ed had said we needed to stay put for another hour or so before we started mop-up, which was when we went back over the land to make sure the fire was going out. So I stepped aside and called Amber. She was the eighteen-year-old daughter of one of my old professors, a freshman studying towards a psychology degree while on a basketball scholarship. I'd failed to put Finn on any daycare waitlists early enough—as in, months before he was born— and she was the only childcare we'd been able to secure once I returned to work. She'd been taking care of Finn a few afternoons a week since the fall semester, an arrangement that wasn't ideal, but which still afforded me some minor freedoms. She had a test the next day, she reminded me now, otherwise, she was happy to watch Finn a while longer. She might try and study while Finn played if that was okay.

'He likes clementines,' she said.

'He does,' I said.

Ed was beckoning to me to hurry up.

'He keeps begging for more,' Amber said. 'He calls them 'oranges', at least I think that's what he's saying.'

'Sounds great,' I said, and I hung up.

I should have listened to all the parts of myself that were telling me I shouldn't be out there. I should have returned to my job of taking care of my son. I should have found some courage and left.

While I scratched away at the earth with Ed's rake, I was both focusing with a furiousness on what I was doing and also thinking distractedly about Dan. I couldn't for the life of me understand why I hadn't told him about the burn. The stupidity of the secret felt huge. I thought about Dan's question from the day we met Gray. *Are you even attracted to me anymore?* I still couldn't get over the fact that he had asked me this point blank. It wasn't like him to be so direct, and that had continued to bother me almost more than the content of the question and my response. That final word: *anymore.* There was something particularly disappointing about it. I'd felt it hanging between us since that afternoon as if it were a concrete thing, a rock that had been thrown into the air and now remained unnaturally suspended just out of reach. My mind, it was too much elsewhere and spinning on this, and I think that was how I managed to get so close to the body before I saw it.

I smelled it first—a smell that I can only place on reflection because at the time it was mingled with the other unusual scents of the day. I remember this faraway thought descending on me as I turned over my concerns about Dan—what's that smell? That's gross and different—and then there was the body, and I was too close not to see it.

It was lying in a sandy clearing between pine trees. The earth around it was a hot carpet of black and grey and brown. Though it made no sense, I briefly believed the person to still be alive. From where I was standing I could tell they were lying face down with their hands nestled under their chest—though maybe that wasn't exactly right, the body still being at some distance from me and obscured by the smoke. But I was close enough to see that however long they had been lying in the forest, exposed to the elements and animals and insects, they had been reduced to bones and partially decomposed meat. The fire also appeared to have licked free most of the fabric of their clothes. The thing that made my brain flicker briefly from the horror of the real into the horror of the uncanny was the movement of the body, which itself wasn't moving, rather there was a sense of movement because of the rolling of the smoke and what I later learned were wasps and beetles not wildly bothered by the last of the smoke and the heat, making a final go of what was palatable, hurrying in and around what remained of the body, navigating its loosening as if the spaces were corridors, windows, doors.

I was so shocked by what I saw that I think it created a short circuit in my system. I remember screaming at the top of my lungs, except I would learn later that wasn't what had happened at all. If I was yelling it was only in my head. What really happened was Fran, who had been shovelling the earth about twenty yards from me and who had been regularly calling out that I should move this way or that way, looked up from what she was doing to give me a new direction, and saw me standing with a stillness that, she said, made her shoot up vertical out of her own skin. As she drew near, she saw my eyes were closed. She called to me, but I didn't respond and so she moved closer, and that's when she saw the body too.

'Oh my Lord,' she said. 'Oh my Lord.'

I don't remember my eyes being shut. I do remember Fran saying that. She called out to Ed next, who picked up the radio first and his phone next without saying a word to either of us.

'Is it the boy,' Fran said. 'The missing one?'

I wanted to run away, but I couldn't. I couldn't even turn

around. It was as if I'd been turned to stone. I could feel my body, its parts, but I couldn't will them to do anything.

Fran reached out and took me by the arm. It was a firm grip that I can still sense now—the spread of her fingers, how violent it was, how I appreciated that. She pulled me away so that I was no longer looking at the body, though that didn't matter anymore because the image of it had already taken residence in my head.

Fran returned to mop-up. I could hear her saying to herself, 'Gotta keep doing it, gotta keep doing it,' over and over.

I knew immediately that it was Calvin.

He was one of the engineering students I'd taught technical writing to the previous fall semester. He had been missing for nearly a month. Earlier in the week his shoes had been found near another stretch of forest a few miles away. The news article had been accompanied by the same photograph of Calvin that had been in circulation since January—his official university baseball portrait, with his cap pulled down low over his brow, his pinstripe team shirt crisp and white, his smile wide. Even if I'd been able to conjure that photo in that moment in the forest, none of those things were reflected in what I could see lying so close to me. Yet, somehow, I knew it was him, as if someone had spoken the words directly into my ear. *Calvin Medina.* Perhaps that was what it felt like to be visited by God.

'Gotta do what needs to be done,' Fran was saying. 'Good Lord, good Lord.' She was repeating these phrases in a low singsong voice, like you might use for a nursery rhyme. Like the song 'Five Green and Speckled Frogs' Dan and I had first learned at Music & Movement and that we sang when Finn was fussing on the changing table—shushing, calming.

'Gotta do what needs to be done,' Fran said. 'Good Lord, good Lord.'

A grisly scene, that's what it was. A phrase I'd learned from watching too many crime shows, from seeing this kind of thing on a screen too often, which was nothing like seeing it for real. A grisly scene. Once I hooked onto it, I couldn't let it go. Grisly. The section of my brain that was trying to keep this ship afloat needed to label what it had seen.

'Gotta do it, gotta keep doing it,' Fran sang.

Grisly, grisly, grisly, I thought.

Then I thought, Yes, grisly, but also gristly. And though it had been rising up from the first moment, it was the picture of that word that made me throw off my hard hat, plant my gloved hands firmly on my knees and vomit.

Once I'd cleaned out my guts, I moved myself outside of the burn site, sat down on the ground and waited. I couldn't see the body. I'd started to shake—my initial possessed state now cresting as a massive wave of terror energy. I would like to say that I took up my rake and, like Fran, continued to turn the earth, but I wasn't that strong. Instead, I buried my head between my knees and focused on the simple act of breathing, which had suddenly become a mammoth task. That's how I remained till the police arrived.

Fran's instincts turned out to be correct—not disturbing the scene, but smothering the fire, to create a clearing for all the people who would want to look and take photographs, to begin to investigate, and to eventually deliver the body back to its family. Calvin. His body. His family.

I called Dan. He didn't pick up.

I called my friend Chantelle. Her phone was off.

A male detective recorded my contact details. He was brusque, humourless. Over his shoulder I could see Ed and Gerry finishing the mop-up we had started. The fire was

41

almost all out. All I wanted to do was go home, to my son, to my husband. Maybe sensing this, the detective explained that one of his colleagues would call me tomorrow to arrange a time for an interview, which was routine in situations like this. He stepped to the side and pointed in the direction of a woman with a blond ponytail who was standing beside where Calvin's body lay covered in a yellow plastic sheet. The woman was wearing black pleated dress-pants, a short-sleeved white blouse and black leather boots. Even though she was wearing sunglasses, and despite the smoke and the glare of the low afternoon sun, I recognised her as the mother of one of the kids who attended the same Music & Movement session as Finn. Her name was Loren. I'd seen her just the day before, when she had insulted Chantelle and her son, Wren, over some plastic stacking cups. Though neither Loren nor I indicated that we knew each other, I thought briefly of that exchange, which had left Chantelle fuming. Back in the days of Baby Lap Time, pre-Music & Movement, Loren had spent the majority of the sessions burping her son. I never once saw that kid feed, but every week for the longest time I saw him being burped.

Out there in the forest I therefore found myself with the image of Loren's large, bell-shaped son stretched awkwardly across her lap, the heel of her hand meeting his back, *whack-whack*, while his tongue hung from his wet mouth and jiggled, till the final blow that freed him of all that gas, his body erupting with a shudder, a thin dribble of milk sliding from his mouth unnoticed on to the carpet.

I could hear Finn before I knocked. When Amber opened the door to the house she still lived in with her parents, I saw him standing by the glass sliding door on the other side of the living

42

room, the door that led to the backyard and the swimming pool. The pool was wide and clean. I'd swum in it once, years ago, at a Fourth of July cookout. I'd spent most of that party in and around the water, drinking beer after beer, Dan bringing me hotdogs on a paper plate, the smooth brown skins of the buns peeling off onto my wet fingers. The sun was high and hot that day. It had been a perfect time. Now the sun was throwing long shadows across the surface of the pool. At the edge of the garden were several orange trees with deep green leaves, laden with dark fruit. With the sky a dense blue behind them, the scene was stunning, but Florida this time of year, it always seemed off, and could with the slightest twist sadden me. Today, looking at that scene, I felt nothing. I felt like I was looking at a reproduction of a Florida Scene hanging on the wall in my dentist's waiting room. When Finn turned around he looked at me blankly, as if he didn't know who I was.

I'd called Dan twice more—once before I left the forest, and again on the way to Amber's. I wasn't sure I could drive without throwing up or passing out or falling into a puddle of fright. When Dan didn't pick up or call me back, there was nothing else to be done.

'Hey, sweetie,' I said to Finn. I was trying to behave as normally as possible.

When I was a few feet from him, he finally broke into a wide grin. He pointed at the door and did his best to name it: 'Door.'

Recently, a woman at the supermarket had said that Finn trying to speak sounded like he was falling down a flight of stairs. With his second birthday just over a week away, I knew the time was coming when Dan and I would need to address his speech development head-on. At Finn's last vaccine appointment, his paediatrician had mentioned it less as something that immediately needed to be actioned, and more of a *let's watch this space*. He still spoke so infrequently, and if the words did arrive, they always tumbled in on that frothing wave. They were little boats in a storm being pitched into the darkness and I was the lighthouse back on shore trying to catch the shape of them in a beam of light that was never quite strong enough. It was exhausting and I feared more than anything that Finn could sense that in me.

'Yes,' I said, with as much warmth as I could muster, 'that's the door.'

'It's time to feed Mac and Cheese,' Amber said. 'If Finn wants to help?'

Amber looked like a freshman college ball player. She was six feet tall, blonde and shiny. Her hair was always done in tight twin braids, the sharp tail of each reaching her shoulder blades.

'I'm sure he'd love to,' I said, picking up Finn. I nuzzled my face into his neck and made a happy growling animal noise. 'Wouldn't you?'

Mac and Cheese were the pet tortoises who lived in the small courtyard in the centre of the house. Mac was the one with the outgoing personality. He would eat a slice of strawberry straight from the palm of your hand. Cheese liked to spend a lot of time hiding under the house. Amber took Finn from me and lugged him into the courtyard, closing the glass sliding door behind her. The two of them squatted down beside the pond in the middle of the courtyard, Mac and Cheese's pond, and Amber placed the plate of water-soaked pellets on the ground, then piled it high with supermarket arugula. I moved closer and bent my fingers against the door handle.

'Here comes Mac,' I could hear Amber say. 'You want to give him a pat?' Mac came running as fast as his legs would carry him. 'That's right, Finn, nom noms for Mac.' Amber turned to look at me, grinned.

On the far side of the pond was a dull brass water feature of a dolphin that was about twenty inches tall. It was suspended mid-leap above a waterfall that fell some ten inches into the pond. Water shot in an arc from the dolphin's blowhole—that was the main event. It made a messy splash as it hit the surface of the pond. There was also water dripping from the dolphin's open mouth. It wasn't clear if the fountain was meant to do that, or if it had sprung a leak. There was nothing majestic about this detail. It looked as if the dolphin was drooling. A creature not in control of itself.

I didn't know what to do with what I'd seen. I'd left the forest in an oddly calm state in the end. I was so desperate to get away that being able to physically remove myself from the scene didn't exactly bring relief, but it smoothed out the worst of it so that I could get behind the wheel of the car and safely, sanely, say to myself, that's not my life, this, what I'm driving towards now, is my life.

Not that, this.

As I watched Amber and Finn, I became freshly overwhelmed, not with grief but fear. It was a picture: Amber demonstrating how to gently stroke Mac's shell while Mac went to town on the arugula, and my boy, Finn, that vessel of hopes and dreams and life yet to be lived—god, some days it killed me to think of all the things he had yet to experience and how if I was lucky I would get to witness it all from the sidelines, the marvel of his little life—here he was following Amber's lead and gently prodding the tortoise's hard shell, and he was smiling and loving every second of it. Being a parent was like living your life from a flying trapeze. The view, the thrill of it, that part was unmistakable. Now, though, as I watched my son, and I saw his broken top teeth flash as he laughed, saw the flop of his dark hair catch against his eyebrows, saw his chubby hands discoloured with the juice of all those clementines, saw him turn from Mac to face me, his mother, in the back of my mind a new terrible thought bloomed: What if it was taken away? How far down was the drop really?

4.

For a minute I would forget what had happened and everything would feel normal. Then the memory of it would clear a space in me with a sudden violence like the punch of an umbrella being opened in my chest. I didn't want it in there—the umbrella, that feeling. To distract myself on the way home from Amber's, I'd wound down the windows and chatted nonsense to Finn. Though as I struggled up our front steps with Finn wedged against my right hip, my bag and Finn's diaper bag on my left shoulder, I started to feel full of it and I wobbled under its weight. I thought I might be sick again.

A blue mountain bike was locked to the railing on our front porch. It belonged to our friend Perry. Dan's red road bike would be locked up in the backyard. Dan and Perry were in the living room. They were a couple of beers in, judging by the empties on the coffee table. Jazz piano was playing on the stereo. Both men were sitting forward in their chairs, elbows on their knees, their faces obscured by the peaks of their caps, staring at a game of backgammon. I saw a Bud Powell record sleeve propped up on the floor beside Perry's chair.

'We're here,' I said, as brightly as I could muster. I dropped the bags to the floor.

Perry, a South Carolinian, immediately stood to greet me. Like Dan and me, he was in his mid-thirties. He adjusted his cap, smiled. At least four of his teeth had gold crowns, and he wore them like a ram wears his horns.

'You're home late,' Dan said, leaning back in his chair. He wasn't chastising me, more stating fact. He looked curious.

'We are,' I said.

'There's my boy,' Dan said, extending his arms to Finn. 'How was your day?'

I didn't answer. Neither did Finn who, as he ran to his father, reached out—the length of his arms constantly surprised me—and swiped half the backgammon pieces out of place.

'Bud, no,' Dan said, as he pried a game piece from Finn's hands.

Finn started to howl. It was late and he was hungry and it was my fault.

'He's all right,' Perry said. He handed Finn one of his pieces. 'I was dead in the water, little dude.'

Finn gripped the biscuit of wood like his life depended on it, and relaxed back into Dan's chest. I loved seeing Finn like that—with his father. I'd been paying closer attention to these moments recently, the happy picture of Finn and Dan without me.

'Can I get you a cold drink?' Perry asked.

'In a minute maybe, Perry,' I said. 'Thanks.'

'Dan's instructing me in the fine art of backgammon,' Perry said.

Dan had tried to teach me how to play years ago, not long after we first started living together. As a teacher he was patient for the most part, but he wasn't systematic in his explanations or his memory of how the game went. Every time we played he recalled a new rule, so that after a while I'd wondered if he was making it all up so he could keep winning. Backgammon had become an odd bone of contention in our household.

'Really?' I said. Usually I would make fun, unable to hide my scepticism, but today this was all I could manage.

'She's just bitter because she could never beat me,' Dan said, not picking up on my tone. He was smirking in a loving kind of way.

'Did you get my missed calls?' I said.

Dan looked at me blankly. 'No?' he said, in the way that he did when he had no idea where his phone was.

'I was saying to Dan,' Perry said, tapping on the edge of the backgammon board, 'that he should make more of these and sell them.'

Before we received our green cards, when I was still a grad student and Dan's spouse visa meant he wasn't allowed to work, he had found odd, under-the-table jobs, gardening and house painting mostly, though he'd also done some work for a furniture maker. It was this last gig that had resulted in a career change, so that, when we returned to Florida with our permanent resident visas, he didn't look for architecture work, but instead got an apprenticeship with the furniture maker. The hours were long and variable. This wasn't a problem—I was happy for him to be doing something he loved. In this way, we had always supported each other.

Dan had made the backgammon board after-hours at work a while back, with mitres for the corners and dados for the internal partitions—*mitres and dados*, the language of his work and interests slowly burrowing its way into the language of our life. He'd carefully painted on the shapes and coloured the game pieces using milk paint. It was a lovely object, anyone could see that. Though I was reminded now of the evening Dan had first introduced me to this project. He'd arrived home much later than expected to find me struggling through another breastfeeding session with Finn. He'd kissed me hello, then dug around in his pocket in such a way that I thought he might have a gift for me. He held out his hand, revealing a round disc of wood with chiselled grooves on top, coloured a pale watery yellow, so it looked like a shortbread cookie.

'This is what you've been doing?' I'd said.

'For a bit,' he'd said. Then either not hearing or choosing to ignore my scolding tone he'd added, 'It looks cool, right?' before sliding it back into his jeans pocket.

That conversation, it was nothing. It was in the past and it was small and it wasn't worth a thing. Yet, recalling it, I felt the swelling of something bad.

'You could travelling-salesman the sets to all the retirement homes of Florida,' Perry said.

'That's actually not a stupid idea,' Dan replied. He looked at me hopefully. 'What were you calling about?' He leaned forward, picked up his beer, took a swig, before he rocked back into his chair and wrapped both arms tightly around Finn. 'You didn't say how your day was.'

I didn't know how to begin.

'Been a challenging one?' Perry said.

He leaned back into his chair too, and put his hands behind his head. In the time we'd known him he'd become a thicker man. Dan thought it was the result of replacing smoking with trips to Popeyes, though that looked like only part of it to me. Under his warm and outgoing front, for that was what you got with Perry most of the time, it seemed to me like he'd lost something—a treasure—and that he'd given up looking for it. It reminded me of what I'd been like before I met Dan, which filled me with sadness, as well as a tug of regret.

'I spent the afternoon down in the forest,' I said. I sounded lighthearted and earnest, like someone desperate to get to the punchline of a joke. I needed to sit down. My legs didn't feel good.

'What forest?' Dan said. 'I thought I saw a raccoon in the yard.'

'You have raccoons?' Perry said. 'You remember the plague of them in my last house, the whole family living up there in the ceiling.' He lifted his arms above his head in disbelief. 'Once they're in, there's no gettin' them out.'

'Were Animal Control no help?' Dan asked. He lowered Finn to the ground.

Perry shrugged. 'I also had armadillos under the floor, the termites swarming every summer, the goddamn fleas.' He drifted off into the disgust of this memory. 'It was a horrible, horrible place to live.'

'Termites,' Dan said, thoughtfully, as if he were making a mental note.

'I didn't see any animals,' I said.

I was still standing in the middle of the living room. Neither man was looking my way. I sat down on the floor. No, I needed to go further. I rolled over and lay down on my side. I could see beneath the couch and the chairs where Dan and Perry were sitting. We hadn't cleaned under there since moving in, and there was an infestation of crumbs, dust, hair, Duplo blocks, the equivalent of an entire one-and-a-half sandwiches of cut triangles, a teaspoon, a fork, three tiny socks, four cockroach corpses, and a board book we'd borrowed from the library and for which, when I'd confessed it was lost, the librarian—Jason—had cancelled the fines.

Dan stood and walked to where I was lying on the floor. He bent down, placed his hand on my shoulder and peered into my face. 'What's going on?' he said.

I'd recently seen a toddler at Music & Movement do something like this. The brown-haired boy—he wasn't a regular—had somehow got himself tangled up in his play scarf, and though he was clearly upset, he didn't yell or cry, but lay quietly facedown on the carpet, arms by his side, all while still cocooned in the purple fabric, and radiated disappointment. I'd thought it the most dismal sight—a two year old self-flagellating in this way. I shouldn't have been lying on the floor either. It wasn't a good look, but I was still partly in shock. Arriving home, touching down on familiar, solid land, I'd felt a sense of security that so wholly contrasted with what I'd seen in the forest. *Not that, this.* These two things—my body in my home, and the body that I could see in my mind—they didn't go together. It was doing something to my wiring.

'I don't know,' I said.

I thought I could fall asleep right there on the floor. I wondered if I was fainting, if the lack of water was finally catching up with me and if what I desperately needed was an IV drip of fluids and a proper lie down in a hospital bed while someone watched over me.

'Is your back sore again?' Dan asked.

It was a question meant kindly. The origin of my back pain was a minor accident from when I was a teenaged volunteer lifeguard at the beach where I grew up. It still bothered me from time to time, especially when I spent long periods standing or sitting, or lifting and carrying Finn. There had been times when it was bad enough that all I could do was lie on the floor. So Dan asking me this was grounded in history. Yet it still bugged me immensely that he was so off base, that he wasn't able to see what was really going on. What was the point of being with someone for eight years if they couldn't figure some things out on their own?

'My back's fine,' I said. The frustration in my voice was clear. I stood up. 'I need to get Finn's dinner together.'

In the kitchen I turned on the faucet and poured myself a glass of water that I drank in desperate gulps. I filled another glass and drank half of that too. The fridge was chocka with plastic containers of leftovers, cut fruit, roasted vegetables, and other meals and snacks I'd cooked in bulk for Finn. I removed what I thought was a Finn-sized serving of pasta with cannellini beans, one of his least-rejected dinners. I was on the cusp of losing it completely, and I didn't want to. I thought that if I could get Finn fed, then I could go for a long walk by myself, followed by a long shower, and that those things back-to-back would make me feel better. I placed the container of food in the microwave and turned it on just as Dan appeared beside me.

'Are you okay?' he said. 'Talk to me.'

'Do I look okay?' I said.

He moved closer so I had to crane my neck to meet his eyes. He was wearing an old heather-grey T-shirt with an unbuttoned flannel shirt over the top. Both were sporting a fine coat of sawdust. This was his natural state, now. I wanted so much to fold myself against his barrel-like chest.

'Talk to me,' he said again.

He reached out, placed his hand to the back of my head, and swept me towards him. I didn't put my arms around him, but I did submit. I couldn't remember the last time we'd hugged, or even semi-hugged like this. I could feel Dan's heart beating, slowly at first, then quickening. I became aware that I was shaking. I felt chilled, as if we were standing in the freezer section at Publix after someone had opened all the freezer doors wide.

'Oh my god,' I said.

'You smell like smoke,' Dan said.

I closed my eyes and saw that smoke.

'Something terrible happened,' I said. I was speaking into Dan's chest. 'There was a person in the forest. They were dead. There was almost nothing left of them. Wasps were eating them.'

'Someone was dead?' Dan said. 'Is that what you said?'

'It was Calvin,' I said.

'I can't hear you,' Dan said. He pulled back from me.

'It was Calvin,' I said again.

'Who's Calvin?' Dan said.

Dan's failure to understand what I was trying to say, though what I was saying was out of the blue and packed with many surprising elements, made me feel like what I'd experienced that afternoon was something I'd dreamed up and that my inability to make him understand stemmed from the fact of its unrealness. I felt oddly at ease for a moment, as if part of my brain was taking Dan's side and had decided that it was nonsense and that I should let it go.

The microwave beeped just as I felt my phone buzz in my pocket. It was Chantelle. Without thinking about what I was doing, I declined her call. I sometimes wonder how differently things might have gone had I taken a breath and accepted that call. These invisible little forks, they're everywhere in the road. Instead, I stepped away from Dan, wadded up a tea towel and retrieved the container, which I placed on the kitchen counter. Dan moved so he was standing directly behind me.

'This isn't good,' I said, the words arriving in a calm manner, as I removed the still-scalding lid on Finn's dinner. 'I'm not good.'

'What're you doing with my eggs?'

It was Dan's tone, I think, that made me feel so accused, rather than what he said. I was looking down at the container of hot eggs, but I was back in the forest. I was standing within view of Calvin's body, and I could smell him, but it was Jason who burrowed his way into my thoughts. He hovered above it all, and I mentally drew a red line from him to the forest and Calvin. It all started rising back up, and I thought I would be sick again. But it burst forth in a different way, with a swell of adrenalin and I heard myself curse with a low bone-cracking whisper as the swell crested.

The plastic container I'd removed from the microwave wasn't the kind we usually bought from Walmart, but a retro Tupperware rip-off I'd found at the Goodwill, having been intoxicated by the citrus colours of the opaque plastic. I should have checked its contents, at least cracked the lid, before I put it in the microwave. Or, on learning too late that I'd picked up Dan's eggs, which he liked to make in two-day batches for his egg-salad sandwiches, I should have left them be. Instead, and this all happened in a second, I picked up the container and threw it and its contents into the kitchen sink with force. That the old and brittle plastic broke as it did shouldn't have been surprising—though I have since also learned something

55

about not putting hardboiled eggs in the microwave, how the heat from the eggs collects under the shell and has nowhere to go. But when the eggs, on hitting the stainless-steel sink, exploded, and the plastic container splintered, I had no idea what was happening. I thought the explosion was happening in my brain. I put my hands to my head.

'Help,' I said, dumbly.

At the same time, Dan started loudly cursing. I turned around to find he'd thrown off his glasses and was covering his right eye with one hand.

Perry soon appeared in the kitchen with Finn on his hip. Finn stared at his father, then at me. He extended his arms.

'Come here,' I said. 'You're okay.'

'What happened?' Perry said. The way he looked at me wasn't all kindness.

'Nothing,' I said. I was in a state of confusion. The whole thing was disorienting.

Dan removed his hand from his eye. He blinked. 'Nope,' he said. He turned and walked up the stairs.

Perry and I exchanged a look. Then, with Finn on my hip, I followed Dan into the bathroom, where he'd folded himself down over the sink and was with some difficulty running cold water over his eye.

'Is it gone?' I said.

I put Finn down. He immediately went for his bath toys.

Dan stood up and blinked hard a few times. 'I think so.'

'Thank god,' I said.

Finn had picked up the bottle of bubble bath from the end of the tub. He did his best to say it: 'Bubble?'

'No bubbles right now,' I said.

'Nope,' Dan said, still blinking. He went back under.

It can't have been comfortable twisting himself into that position under the tap. I've since had to do something similar with Finn, when on a late summer day I entered the living room to find him bawling and holding a canister of roach spray with his eyes screwed shut. I sprinted across the room and without stopping, scooped him up, letting the canister fall, and in a matter of seconds had positioned him under the tap in the kitchen sink.

'What do you think it was?' I said to Dan. 'Was it plastic? It'd be weird if it was a bit of eggshell.'

Dan didn't respond.

'What can I do?' I said. I attempted to use my hands to direct the water from the tap more precisely in the direction of Dan's eye.

'Bubble?' Finn said.

'No bubbles, sweetie,' I said.

'I think that's helping,' Dan said. 'Let me check. Hold on.'

As Dan stood, I angled another handful of water at his eye but somehow too vigorously so it mostly went up his nose. He began spluttering.

'You trying to waterboard me?' he said.

I would unintentionally do the same to Finn the day with the roach spray, and he would similarly start spluttering till I pulled him out from under the tap and held him upright, both his eyes open—that part seemingly okay—and patted his back and jiggled him. He would cough and sob and all I would think was *dry drowning*, and how hard it was to do any of this right.

Dan had removed a towel from the towel rack and was dabbing at his face. He coughed twice more, though it seemed put on to me—his way of driving home the fact that not only was I the one who had caused this mess but in the aftermath I was no help.

'I'm really sorry,' I said.

'Hmm,' Dan said. He blinked a few more times, then leaned down so his face was on my level. He lifted his eyelid with a finger. 'Can you see anything?'

I looked closely. The white part of his eye was red, though he'd been rubbing it and showering it with tap water. I couldn't see anything else, nothing alarming, no gashes or fragments of eggshell sticking out.

'It's red,' I said, 'but that's all.'

'How red?' Dan said.

'Not too red,' I said. 'It's not bleeding if that's what you mean.'

During this time Finn had not relented in his request for bubbles. He'd been saying the word over and over, each pronouncement framed by his usual rush of noise, creating a horrible buzzing in the back of my head. He was holding the pink bottle of bubble bath up to me with a determined and righteous expression on his face.

'No,' I said. 'No bubbles.'

'There's no need to yell at him,' Dan said, throwing the towel down by the basin.

Sometimes with Dan I felt like I was standing on the wrong side of a closed door. I could hear him and I knew he was there, but it was muffled, and maybe he really wasn't there, maybe it was a tape recording of his voice I was hearing, or the wind in the goddamn trees. That wind, it wasn't listening to me. I picked up the towel Dan had tossed beside the basin. 'I guess I'll put this away,' I said.

'Jesus Christ,' Dan said

'No, not Jesus Christ,' I said.

'Bubble?' Finn said.

'No fucking bubbles,' I said.

I snatched up the bottle from Finn's hands and in the same breath attempted to sling Dan's towel back over the towel rack, except I did this with such force, and with the towel all bunched up, that the screws fastening the rack to the soft drywall were outmatched, and the whole thing came crashing down at my feet.

The room fell silent.

Finn was the first to speak: 'Oh no.'

Dan escorted Finn from the bathroom and I thought of the time I threw the backgammon board and its pieces out the sliding door and into the rain-soaked yard. Dan wasn't home, and I couldn't for the life of me recall what would have made me do such a thing—to single out the board and pick it up and carry it to the door and open the door and then hiff it into the air. I'd eventually collected the board and pieces from where they lay scattered across the yard, towelled the lot of it down and arranged it all in a sunny place to dry. By the time Dan arrived home, the set had looked fine, and it was as if it had never happened.

Once Perry went home and Dan took Finn upstairs to bed, I put on my trainers and left the house. My evening walks had begun out of necessity. Finn needing to be pushed to sleep in the stroller for hours day and night was something I'd been readied for after witnessing the haunted performances of mothers real and fictional, and for months I'd endured it, thinking it the only way and a rite of passage. When Finn eventually resigned himself to his crib, which is to say Dan and

I sleep-trained the hell out of him, I found myself missing those walks. Not the daily, many hours of them, but being out in our neighbourhood, especially in the twilight, not going anywhere in particular, just around. It was a small pleasure that I could have and so most evenings this was something Dan gave me— time to walk alone.

I wanted to tell Jason about what had happened. The desire to see him and for him to lean into me with comforting words and touch was big, but I didn't have the slightest idea of how he might actually respond to my appearing unannounced at his door. I wished I could ball up that uncertainty, stuff it into my pocket, and just go. Instead, I walked not towards Jason's, which was on the opposite side of the stream and artifical pond that divided our neighbourhood, but south, taking a route that led to nothing important. I didn't put in my earbuds, but listened to the sounds of the neighbourhood: all the swimming pool heaters and pumps; all the shrieking squirrels; a pair of young children driving alone on the sidewalk in a pink child-sized SUV, radio blasting; a woman explicitly trimming a spiky shrub.

As I reached the southernmost point of my walk, I turned and headed towards the old army barracks that had been converted into units, the low U-shape of their arrangement reminding me of a long-ago school camp. I passed a two-storey house hemmed in by huge plaster ionic columns, and a spooky brick cottage that from a distance looked like it was made of gingerbread. As I crossed the road, something blinking sharp in the evening light caught my eye. It was a stainless-steel fork someone had stabbed into the trunk of a sabal palm. A drunk person had put it there probably, a student likely. I don't know what it was about that sight, but it made me think again of those scarred hills from my childhood. The feeling I had while witnessing their destruction—I dug around and discovered that it was still in there too.

The blocks I'd put between myself and Dan and Finn hadn't filled me with any of the usual cheer and lightness. Instead it had stirred in me a deep dread. Dan and I had moved to Florida because we wanted a different kind of life to the one we'd been living in New Zealand. Around us, all of our friends were rapidly blooming into the exact people I'd anticipated, and that had scared me. I'd not been fleeing anything, I'd only wanted to not be able to guess exactly how my life would look five, ten, twenty years down the line. I'd wanted the murkiness and potential of a Florida swamp. There were no dead bodies in New Zealand though. Not a single person in New Zealand ever died. Here, the forests probably were overflowing with decomposing corpses, and who knew, maybe I hadn't found Calvin, but some other person, while Calvin was still out there waiting to dig out someone else's brain and heart with a blunt wet trowel.

I came upon an odd-looking blue and white house then. I'd not noticed this house before. It had a façade with a distinct chalet-in-the-mountains air. It was a house for a horror movie where the whole ski-loving family are slaughtered in a way that isn't unique but cinematically about maximum blood against snowy white canvas. It was a house that didn't belong in Florida. A coldness crept up my spine. I jumped and looked over my shoulder, but the street was empty save for a pair of crows.

'Oh, it's just you guys,' I said.

I didn't like hearing my voice. It cracked and it sounded wrong. I turned on my heels, and with my heart in my mouth

I hurried back home.

'Finn go down okay?' I asked Dan when I got in the door.

I was wheezing and sweating, having broken into a jog for the last few blocks. I'd never been a runner. Dan was sitting on the couch holding his Xbox controller. There was no time I found him less attractive than when he was doing this, on the edge of his seat, legs spread, eyes two glazed donuts.

He didn't immediately reply.

'Huh?' I said. 'Did you hear what I said?'

Between us hung the sounds of the explosions on the screen and the *tap-tap* of the controller as it responded to Dan's touch, and that was all.

Dan didn't look at me when he finally spoke: 'There were no issues.'

5.

'It doesn't need thickening,' Dan said.

At the click of my unfastening the lid of the slow cooker he'd appeared in the kitchen. I was hovering over his stew with the wooden spoon and a bag of flour. I'd slept for no more than three hours, and I was doing my best to continue on like everything was fine.

'It seemed thin,' I said.

Last week Dan had had a craving for the kind of stew we usually cooked in the depths of winter, though temperatures were in the eighties now and it was the last thing I wanted to eat. Still, I'd bought the ingredients, anticipating coming home and throwing the lot in the slow cooker, except Dan had expressed a wish to make it. It had been a long time since he'd offered to cook anything, so this had pleased me. Then the ingredients had languished in the fridge till late last night when I was about to turn out the lights and get into bed and I finally heard Dan sharpening the chef's knife.

Dan was a product of a childhood brain that enjoyed making and painting model aeroplanes and the tiny human figurines meant to accompany them. He liked work that was precise and finicky, and this was how he treated his food preparation— though I was paradoxically the tidier of us. Dan reached past me and gently stirred his immaculately prepared vegetables and horrifyingly precise cubes of meat. The house was full of the stench of it, and, though I was trying to butt in and take charge, my stomach was also churning with the proximity.

'I'm going to add a bit,' I said, rolling open the bag of flour.

That morning, there was some lightness in the air, a stillness that made me think of a Florida lake on a cool winter morning.

'Give it some body,' I said.

'*No body*. This stew'—Dan stopped for a moment, blinking hard, and clearly with discomfort—'it has a delicate flavour.'

'A delicate flavour? You sound like your dad.'

'*It has a delicate flavour*,' Dan said, investigating. 'Yes, I guess I do.' He smiled. He'd decided to own this comment. He put his finger to his eye.

'Don't rub it,' I said.

The night before, after I'd arrived back from my panicked walk, I'd showered and come back downstairs to find Dan had switched off his Xbox. I'd found myself increasingly mortified by Perry's witnessing of the evening's events. On top of everything else, I hated letting someone else in on the theatre of our marriage. I'd apologised to Dan then, for the eggs, for the towel rack, and we had turned to face each other and properly inspect the damage. We each had a single graze, and Dan's right eye was still irritating him, but we both found some energy to laugh about it. Dan made a joke about having egg on his face, and it had felt nice for a moment, even if there was no great relief in it.

'Tell me about what happened today,' Dan had said next. 'In the forest. We never had a chance to talk about it.'

'We don't need to talk about that now,' I'd said.

'Go on,' Dan said. 'I want to know.'

'It was never a secret,' I said. 'I don't want you to think I was keeping it from you.'

'I won't,' Dan said.

'I just never told you. I don't know why.'

'Hmm,' Dan said.

'What does that mean? *Hmm?*'

'It means I'm listening and ready to process.'

I was about ready to throw the camaraderie of the evening out the door. I didn't though, I held on to it tightly and I told Dan how I'd wanted to do this thing for reasons I couldn't quite explain, how I hadn't expected to actually have to do anything on the burn, how the smoke had stung my eyes, how I'd forgotten my water bottle, the thing about the animals having room to shelter, how I'd known immediately that it was Calvin, how Fran had pulled me away, how I'd vomited into the grass, what I'd discussed with the police, how on the way out of the forest, maybe because of the bumpy ride, all those gopher holes, I had to stop the car so I could get out and vomit again. I was unable to tell Dan a single thing about what I'd actually seen of the body, though. When I arrived at that part of the story, I just sat there with my hands clasped in my lap and shook my head.

'I'm not sure what to say,' Dan said, when I was done.

I waited for him to find something else, something better.

'I still reckon it was a frat hazing that went wrong,' Dan said. He'd already shared this theory, when earlier in the week we'd briefly discussed the discovery of Calvin's shoes.

'I don't know if he was in a frat,' I said.

The shoes had been found on the side of the highway just south of the city. Not the interstate, but the older highway that was less frequently used and less well maintained, though for the most part it headed in the same direction. The article about the shoes had reminded readers that as of that time Calvin hadn't been seen for three weeks, and that while finding his shoes might help lead investigators to his body there was otherwise very little hope left. For where could a twenty-year-old have gone and then remained for so long without his shoes? On first reading this, I'd thought, please can no one tell his parents about this discovery. What parent would want to know that their missing kid's shoes had been found minus their kid? What parent could do anything with that?

'Booze, pills, twenty-year-olds who can't handle their booze and pills,' Dan said. 'He probably tried to jump off a roof, tried to jump from a two-storey window into a swimming pool or something.'

'How'd he and his shoes get all the way down there though?' I said.

'That's a mystery.'

'It makes me worry Finn will do something dumb like that.'

I meant the jumping from the roof while drunk and high, or any one of the other scenarios I'd set up in my mind for Finn the twenty-year-old, situations that at their most exotic included the propellers of boats, warm shark-infested waters, the edge of a lake at dusk, and at their most boring, just a house, a pool, a concrete patio, a flight of wooden stairs.

'Me too,' Dan said.

We both sat silently with this fear for a moment.

'Are you okay?' Dan had said finally. 'I'm sorry, my love.'

My love. Those words had jarred me. That's what Dan always called me—what he had called me from the earliest time—and yet the night before, sitting together on our couch and talking about this thing that was the worst thing I'd experienced in my whole small life, those words, the shape and weight of them, they were foreign and baffling to me.

Now, this morning, I watched as Dan—*my love*—protectively cupped his hand over the eye he wanted to rub.

'Do you need to visit a doctor?' I said.

'Can you look again?' he said.

He put down the wooden spoon, and, as he'd done the night before, bent down to my level, held back his eyelid and bugged out his eye. I leaned forward. I could see the outline of his contact lenses, but nothing else.

'It's still a bit red,' I said. 'That's all. Should you be wearing your contact lenses?'

'It'll be fine,' he said. 'The contacts make it feel better.'

'All right,' I said, 'it's your funeral.'

Anxiety rippled beneath the calm of that morning. For starters, I was unable to get my temperature right. Already I'd changed my clothes twice, and had put on and removed a sweater. There had been a brief article about Calvin on the local news site: 'Remains Found in Forest Believed to be Missing Student'. The piece was accompanied by the photograph of Calvin in his baseball uniform, as well as what looked like a stock photo of the forest. Investigators and cadaver dogs had been searching an area of the forest near where Calvin's shoes had been found, and they had speculated that it would have been only a matter of time before they moved west, to the part of the forest where we'd been burning. The article also said the body couldn't be identified by sight. DNA would have to be used. When I finished reading this, I thought, I was there and I saw him. Then I thought, but I'm not there now, and I'd put down my phone and proceeded to make Finn his breakfast, as if that settled it.

'Bud,' Dan said to Finn now, 'you want more bagel?'

It was the last day of classes before Spring Break, which made me think of Gray. He'd left me a voicemail message the night before that I'd yet to listen to or return. I only considered Gray for a moment though, before my thoughts swung back to Calvin. These tight loops had already started to form in my mind, everything finding its way back to the boy in the forest. I didn't want to think about him. I wanted him out of my head so I could focus on the life in front of me: Dan's tall lean figure bowed over the kitchen counter separating two precut bagel halves. But then as I watched Dan press his fingers down into the cut, wriggle it in, I felt as if he was doing it to me, as if he were attempting to separate the space between my ribs.

I noticed two ceramic bowls sitting on the counter overflowing with potato peels, leafy celery offcuts, long noodles of carrot skin, hairy onion nipples.

'Are you making stock with those?' I said, my voice high with fright.

Dan looked at the bowls of scraps as if he'd never seen them before in his life.

'Yes,' he said.

As my arms shot out and I snatched up the bowls, one in each hand, I brushed Dan in the gut. He flinched and I lost a couple of onion skins to the floor. We both watched them fall like fat ugly feathers.

'I was deciding if I would,' Dan said. 'I can take them out.'

'Yes, you can,' I said. 'Yet, you didn't.'

I passed Finn sitting at the kitchen table where he was creating finger drawings out of the water he'd tipped from his bottle onto the tabletop. When I reached the sliding door, I moved to place one of the bowls on the floor so I could free up a hand.

'Here, I'll get it,' Dan said, and there he was suddenly behind me and reaching over my shoulder to slide the door open.

To bend down and place the bowl on the floor and stand back up and open the door and bend back down to pick the bowl up again—it was nothing. But to not have to do all that, for Dan to do what he did so I could step across the threshold without any effort, was how you made a marriage good. I knew that. And yet that morning, Dan's effort, it *felt* like effort, and I felt pressured.

'You can wipe Finn's face,' I said, as I ducked beneath his arm and kicked on my slides. 'There's peanut butter all over the show.'

The apartment we rented was one half of a small, two-storey bungalow. Unusually for our neighbourhood, it was divided vertically, so we had an upstairs and a downstairs. Each duplex had its own front door, but the backyard was a shared space of concrete patio and scrappy grass, accessible through glass sliding doors. This meant that from the yard we could see into our living room as well as our neighbour's living room, where we would occasionally catch a glimpse of the quiet woman in her thirties who lived there. I walked across the yard to where we kept our garbage bins. As I lifted the lid, I was greeted by the warm sour smell inside. It wasn't like what I'd smelled in the forest the afternoon before, but it tapped on a nearby wall in my brain. I tried to breathe through it, not wanting to vomit again. The night before, I'd not been able to eat anything except half an apple. I'd reluctantly eaten a piece of toast that morning, but only because I was worried about getting through classes without fainting. Now I unlatched our garden gate and walked across the thin patch of St Augustine grass between the house and sidewalk. Our fence was high enough that I couldn't see over it. As with the divide of our house, this was unusual for our neighbourhood where most houses had no fences and the front lawns simply sloped from the front porch to the sidewalk or road, or were ringed by those silly white picket fences that came up to your shins. The apartment we'd rented before this had one of those play fences, and I'd liked sitting on our porch and seeing people walk past, and waving and nodding to them—*morning, evening.* The summer we'd briefly returned to New Zealand I was struck by how intent people were there to square off their slice of land from everyone else with high fences, shrubbery, trees, street-facing windows with the blinds pulled. Before we moved to Florida, I would have guessed it was the other way around.

I stood on the sidewalk and breathed. I stretched my arms above my head and I wanted to cry, but I pushed it down and tried to think of good things, like how much I loved this neighbourhood and its morning movements. It was not yet eight and I couldn't hear a single car engine, just the jingle of a dog's collar somewhere nearby. I looked around for signs of the Big Four: cardinals, northern mockingbirds, red-billed woodpeckers, American crows. On a good day you might also spot a red-tailed hawk keeping its distance on a powerline or street sign. I thought that despite what had happened the day before maybe I'd never been so at home in a place as I was here. Walking through the native New Zealand bush in the surrounds of the house I grew up in was something else, but how did it compare to standing in the street in this neighbourhood in Florida where I had no roots, few friends, and no family except for the two people in the rental behind me, and was it a competition?

The egret first appeared at the edge of my vision like a cloud on my eye—something to see the ophthalmologist about. Only when it was directly in front of me, walking down the middle of our street, did I jump back, startled. In the months that followed I would become a person who frightened very easily, shaken by the smallest things: a squirrel hopping across the sidewalk, a leaf falling from a tree, a stick lying in the road, my shadow twisting with the sun from behind me to beside me.

The egret was following the shadow line cast by the house across the street. If I'd seen it the morning before it would have made me smile. Now, the sight of this bird walking as it did with the S of its long neck stretching and retracting with each step, the perfect creepy mechanical balance of it, chilled me to my core.

Before we moved to Florida I researched the things I was most afraid of that I thought I would have to confront on a regular basis. I made screenshots of FAQ lists, Wikipedia facts, and personal blogposts, which I labelled and placed in a folder on my desktop titled, 'Florida Remember'. Over the course of my research I learned that a mixture of vinegar, baking soda and water poured in the right place could repel fire ants. I learned that it was easier to hold an alligator's mouth shut than it was to pry it open. I learned that you could make a temporary dressing for a wound with cobwebs. I learned that anti-venom is best received within four hours of being bitten by a cottonmouth, and that, if left untreated, bodily functions would start to break down over the following two to three days.

I learned what to do if you encounter a panther in the wild: don't run, don't turn your back, don't crouch or bend, make yourself appear larger, throw stuff, be prepared to fight back. I learned that if you find yourself struck down by lightning to get professional medical help as soon as possible. I learned that there are no completely safe places to shelter from tornadoes. I learned that the only protection you can get against your house and you and your loved ones being swallowed by a sinkhole is to add sinkhole coverage to your insurance policy. I learned that the best defence against an active shooter situation is to always be aware of your environment, to take a moment to identify exits and make a plan to run, or, failing that, know where you can hide. There were also the things that weren't really dangerous but that I was still concerned about having to live with: raccoons, opossums, bats, mosquitos, cockroaches. The only birds on my list were owls, since hearing an account of a local dog owner having to remove a broken hook of talon from her fox terrier's back.

To choose to live in a place surrounded by these creatures, these threats, it made me feel like I was living a bold life. Every day I was facing my fears by just being and walking around amongst them. Now I was close enough to the egret that I could see the green circling its eye, and the intense black dot of its pupil. I knew it saw me, and I knew it wasn't bothered by me as I was bothered by it. The low morning light elongated its shadow, somehow lending it more authority.

'I could crush you,' I said to it.

The egret continued on. I watched for as long as it took to clear the end of our street and turn the corner.

As soon as I stepped back inside the house, I heard Dan say,

'Oh, hello.'

He was talking to his stew. He used to use this breathy sigh of a greeting when he saw me, though I couldn't remember the last time he'd done so. I watched as he pulled out a chair and sat with Finn at the table. In the five minutes I'd been gone, he'd got out Finn's Duplo—the plastic pieces spread out across the tabletop, circling Finn's plate of bagel segments. He started adding a door to a wall while Finn, who now loved the word *door* pointed at it and named it for me. The door was from a Batman set that my brother Gerard and his husband had gifted Finn for his first birthday.

'So why didn't you cancel your classes?' Dan said. When he spoke he didn't look at me. He was concentrating on what he was doing, invested in this play with his son.

I was hovering between the kitchen and living room unsure about where to put myself. I was feeling agitated by my encounter with the egret.

It hadn't occurred to me to cancel class. It was something I did so rarely. My teaching schedule this semester was already a mess. Though I was only teaching two classes in person, the other two online, somehow I'd wound up having to be on campus four days. The hassle of cancelling, the rescheduling involved—it wasn't worth it. I also think I felt a duty to be there for Calvin's subject mates. I cared about my work. I wanted to be a good teacher. At the end of the semester when I received my ratings, rankings, and written feedback from my students, it was always black and white how I was doing, and I drew strength from that. It was different to parenting, where I would have to wait another twenty years or more to see if I'd done a good job with Finn, to see if he was a good man. It was also so wildly different to being a partner, where whether or

73

not I'd done a good job would be revealed at the signing of my and Dan's divorce papers, or on one of our death beds. I also needed to spend the day talking to people about other things. Even if the people I was talking to were my students, and the other things were showing them the best way to plan and write their first literature review. That was more attractive to me than having to spend the day alone with my own thoughts.

'Are you going to say anything?' Dan said.

'To my students?' I said, as I walked towards one of the living room chairs.

'Yeah,' Dan said.

Before I could sit down, I saw something, again initially as a white blur out the corner of my eye. It was much smaller than the egret, and stationary, though no less illuminated—a single tissue folded in half and half again and half again, neatly. It was lying on the armrest of the couch. I reached down to pick it up. Over the course of the night its contents had hardened. Dan and I weren't using any contraceptives between us, but with neither of us wanting another kid, on the rare occasions when we stumbled into each other, like a couple of dumb teenagers, we'd taken to using the pull-out method. The last time this had happened, I'd watched Dan wipe up the cum pooling above my pubic line and clean himself, all with a single tissue.

The first thing I wondered was whether Dan had taken time for this after he was done with the stew or if he'd stopped in the middle of chopping vegetables. Though I'd not initially slept when I went to bed, I'd also not been listening carefully to what Dan was up to, it all just a scraping, clanging, rustling white noise of Dan awake and downstairs. I thought of Jason next. I wanted to believe that Jason and I were a separate thing from Dan and me. Even though it was sex, the most important fact was that it was something I was doing for myself, and in that way I still believed it could be substituted with anything, like kayaking, roller-skating, knitting or nature photography, for example.

I held the tissue pinched between my thumb and forefinger. I could take it to the kitchen and watch it fall into the trashcan and not think about it again, or I could stop at the kitchen table where Dan and Finn were playing and say something. I hadn't thought enough about Dan's desires. That was my mistake. The truth of it though was that the tissue did nothing to me, which made me think I should say something, that I should make it matter.

Finn was still going on about the door. On the back of his regular garbled stream, he was saying the word over and over.

'Yes, you're right,' Dan said to Finn. 'Door.'

When he spoke to Finn his tone was even and sincere. He had more patience for this kind of repetition than I did. He was a good dad, a better person than me in a lot of ways really.

'I saw an egret outside,' I said.

'Can you say *egret*?' Dan said. Finn ignored him. Dan turned to me. He winked sharply against the light coming through the sliding doors. 'You didn't say what you were going to say to your students, about Calvin.'

'I'm not going to say a thing,' I said, and slid the tissue into my back pocket.

'That's probably the right course of action,' Dan said.

'I believe so,' I said.

In the time we had been away from New Zealand, a man swimming at the beach where I grew up and where my parents still live, the beach where I'd spent all my time as a kid, first in a recreational sense and then as a volunteer and competitive lifeguard, was, not fifty yards out from the shoreline, attacked and three-quarters consumed by a tiger shark. Which is to say that sometimes it doesn't matter where you are, as no amount of researching, taking notes, looking yourself squarely in the eye and trying to be braver can provide adequate preparation or protection.

6.

When I was in high school, a girl in my classics class committed suicide. Before news of her death spread through our large public girls' school, I was summoned to the health centre with twenty or so other girls, where we were instructed to sit on the floor in a dimly lit room I'd never previously entered. At this point none of us knew what was going on, and I remember running through my head all the things I thought might be about to get me into trouble. All I could come up with was that I'd been caught wearing a black scarf instead of the uniform code navy scarf, for which I'd already received a detention, or that, due to my periods of increased exhaustion from competitive swimming and surf life saving training, I was nearing the maximum number of allowed absences for the school year.

When the headmistress entered the room she didn't pull up a chair, of which there were a few stacked around the walls, but knelt on the floor with us—a strange thing to do for this regal woman in her seventies who still wore flesh-coloured stockings and coordinated skirt suits. After sitting quietly for a moment she said, 'Girls, you're probably wondering what you're doing here.' She paused to acknowledge all the nervous nods. 'You've been asked here because you are friends with Katie and I regret to inform you that she has taken her own life.'

First, it was strange being told I was friends with someone I was not friends with. I struggled to think of a time I'd spoken more than a couple of words to the girl. I'd once travelled with her to a debating event. We'd been on the same team for a single competition, of which the only detail I can recall was that a boy on the opposing Catholic boys' school team knocked over his glass of water, sending it flying across the room and spritzing the judge. After the initial surprise of receiving the news of this girl's death, came a deeper confusion. She had seemed sorted, popular, though also someone who chose her words carefully. She was a good debater, easily the best on our team that day, which was why we didn't see her after that competition; she was promoted to a higher-ranked team. Finally, after the confusion settled, I found myself wanting to laugh. This was the first time in my life I'd encountered true nervous laughter, that welling up of bad feelings manifesting in this entirely inappropriate way. I excused myself promptly, and as the day wore on and word got around the school about what had happened, and my friends wanted to know what I knew, what it had been like sitting in that room, and who had cried, I started to think how the worst thing about this—after the girl's death—was that someone like me had been invited to share in any of it. It haunted me, that dusky room and nervous circle of girls. *You are friends. She has taken her own life.* I wondered who had decided we were the rightful first receivers of this news. Had there been a discussion in the staff room, or had the headmistress had her secretary collect names, or was there a special group of select teachers and coaches who thought they knew the girl best and who had put forward names like some kind of sports draw?

I thought about this during my first class of the day. And on my way to the next, which was in the same building where I'd taught Calvin in the fall, I wondered if a similar thing was happening now in a room somewhere on the university campus. Where a group of adults from Calvin's life, maybe his baseball coach, his careers advisor and RA, probably not the head coach though, likely an assistant coach, a *team representative*, were drawing up a list of people who, once the DNA results landed, got to know first? Or had something like that already been done early on when Calvin first went missing? I never intended to share anything of what had happened in the forest with any of my students, or anyone for that matter, but the more I thought about this, the more I felt it was disgusting to expect anyone to lift up a piece of this horrible thing and then make them carry it around. Telling them, that's what it would do. I wanted no part of that.

As with my first class of the day, the energy of my second was not one of shock or mourning at the discovery of a fellow student's remains. It was a regular Friday vibe, my students part tired, part excited for the weekend, maybe ratcheted a few clicks tighter as they had a whole blissful week of Spring Break ahead.

'I find it interesting,' one of my students was saying, a boy who reminded me of Calvin only because I'd seen them both wearing aviator sunglasses, 'that New Zealand won't let America dock.' He sighed deeply and accusingly. 'America its ally?'

I didn't know that in the last few years a US ship had in fact returned to New Zealand waters, but even if I had, I didn't want to get into a *discussion* with this student. I just wanted to know if he had any questions about the assignment. The nuclear engineering students though, they were cruelly passionate about their chosen field, as if they alone were responsible for turning their fellow citizens and advocating for the whole Nuclear Way.

Calvin had majored in biomedical engineering. I remembered this because, as with the other students on sports scholarships, I had to regularly report to the powers that be whether he was maintaining acceptable grades. Calvin had been a solid A student—not at the very top of the class, but in the front pack. This was something I generally prided myself on, though—learning my students' names, something of who they were, what they wanted. It didn't come naturally to me, recalling so many faces and details. The girls were easier to set apart as they were always more distinct in their dress and personalities, whereas so many of the boys had the same haircuts and dressed in the same university-branded clothes that they formed a frighteningly uniform pack. To get around this, at the start of each semester I drew rough maps of my classrooms, marked where the students sat, and wrote brief physical descriptions and facts. For Calvin I'd written the following: *eyebrows, baseball, left-handed, biomed.* The student I was speaking to now, he was one of a handful of my students who were enlisted. Beside his name I'd written: *navy, buzzcut, freckles, nuclear.* Once he had come to class in his full regalia. Mostly he dressed in university basketball shorts and T-shirt, New Balance trainers and pristine white socks, all of which looked as if they were fresh off the hanger, out of the box.

Now I gave him what I thought he wanted more than a discussion—my approval. 'I get what you're saying,' I said, 'why you find it interesting, now is there anything else?'

'Thanks, Miss Georgie,' he said, sounding both pleased

and worn out.

I couldn't remember being like this when I was an undergrad. So dug in. I was less able to settle and get serious, like a blowfly, as my father frequently told me, jumping from one thing to the next. It was true that whatever I was studying in my English Literature and Education classes was fed by a constant changing stream of other interests. One month I would be trying my hand at stop-motion animation, then I would be throwing myself into the study of metaphysics, then it would be Mahler's symphonies, then playing social soccer five nights a week, then attending Bible classes on Wednesdays and studying scripture at night, then I got really into hiking and agnosticism, then Optimist yachts briefly, Beethoven's Late piano sonatas, atheism, Claire Denis, sprouting a forest of avocado plants from stones suspended above jars of water, dumpster diving, weaving ugly Tapestries out of Found Materials. Many of my students seemed to have already moved beyond this phase of college life, where it had felt to me at least that the world was all there for the taking. They had already settled on what they thought was important and what they would do. Part of me admired their focus, though it also disturbed me how resigned they were to their corners and how sure they were of how the world worked and what it had to offer. I'd been, and still was, much more porous.

I'd spent the first third of the class in lecture mode. Now I was giving the students time to begin researching for their literature review on an engineering topic of their choice. The class was small enough that I had time to check in with each student individually. If the years I'd spent teaching and researching and writing about pedagogy had taught me anything, it was that, even in this pool of students with their huge brains and ambitions, the majority still had questions they would only ask when they were out of earshot of their classmates.

'Professor,' another student said now, as I moved down the aisle.

This one liked to call me professor despite my informing him that I wasn't a professor and I would prefer that he didn't. Next to his name on my class map I'd written: *big kid, dad glasses, chemical.*

'Good afternoon.' He paused to smile politely. 'I like your shirt.'

It constantly surprised me how these kids could be simultaneously so formal and so familiar. There was something about this combination that was particularly American. The shirt was a collared hangover from my breastfeeding days that I wore when nothing better was clean. I thanked the student for his kind comment, and made a mental note to throw the shirt in the trash.

It was then that I heard a crackle. A student in the back of the room was peeling away the wrapper of a Lärabar. It didn't sound much like the crackle of a fire, but in the quiet *tap-tap* of my students hunched over their laptops, I found myself looking around in panic, the fright of the day before rising to the surface.

This classroom, unlike my first room of the day, had no windows. It was in a Nineteen-Sixties era building that had been designed as anti-riot, and so many of the classrooms were of this bunker quality. I didn't know the stats on whether the lack of windows made it safer or not in an active shooter situation, but the two doors, one at each end of the room, were both lockable from the inside. As with every new room I taught in, I'd tested this on the first day of the semester. Hearing that

82

plastic wrapper was I think the closest I'd come to feeling under threat in one of my classrooms.

I steadied myself on a nearby chair back. I'd started to sweat. Though I'd not yet checked in with four of my students, including the one with the Lärabar, I returned to my desk at the front of the class. Ten minutes of the period remained, and that's where I intended to sit for the duration.

Early on in the semester, I had my students share their career goals. This wasn't the awkward icebreaker of my undergraduate years—these kids loved talking about their dreams. Around the same age, my goal had been: move to New York City. Every semester I told my students this and every semester they laughed uproariously. For Calvin's class there were lots of the usual working-for-Google/Boeing/Lockheed ambitions. One student, a thin girl with a persistent cough, wanted to make a living designing roller coasters, and a short, stocky boy who blinked too infrequently was adamant he would become a Navy Seal. Calvin wanted to help create new and better synthetic skins. When he spoke of this, I saw something slide down over his usually steely-cheerful exterior, a sadness or darkness, and it lingered there for a moment, and then it was gone. He didn't give us anything more. Whatever he was thinking about, his motivation for doing a degree in biomedical engineering, if that's what it was, was his alone.

I was thinking about this and about Calvin when one of my students suddenly let out a groan and slumped so completely over her laptop it was as if she no longer contained any structural integrity. My heart began pounding hard and sharp, and I thought, this girl is thinking about Calvin, too, and she's going to expect me to say something of comfort. Next to her name I'd written: *blonde, golf, low talker, electrical.* Some of the students sitting near her began looking from me to her in such a way that it was clear they wanted no part of whatever was going on. I forced myself to get up from my desk and walk across the room. As I squatted down next to her, the girl looked up with fear in her eyes.

'I thought I was going to write about integrated circuits,' she said, 'but now I think I should write about cyber–physical systems. Do you think that's a good idea?' The thing I'd been turning over in my head, an unanswerable question prompted by the memory of the strange shift of Calvin's face that day in class, a day that was memorable only because it came to me now as a bright beacon of his presence in my room, was whether Calvin's short life had been happy. The question gripped me like a hand to the throat. This other student, I wanted to ask her if she had known Calvin, and if she knew how his life had been. And I wanted to go home and kneel down next to my own son and ask him this question too. Finn, I would say, if you died cold and alone in the forest tomorrow night would you say that your life had been a happy life? It occurred to me that even at his young age I couldn't truly know the answer to such a question.

When class finally ended, I wished my students a fun Spring Break, adding, 'Take care out there.' I watched as they stuffed their laptops into their backpacks, gathered up their phones and water bottles, swung past my desk and wished me a Happy Spring Break back, and the overwhelming feeling I got was that it was just another day.

As I switched off the projector and took a final glance around the room before leaving, a student returned.

'Ms Beard?' he said. 'I have some questions.'

Before I could say anything one way or another, he pulled

up a chair and sat at the end of my desk. He took out his laptop and turned the screen to face me.

'I'm applying for summer internships,' he said. 'I know it's late, but it's taken me a while to get here.'

He was what passed as a mature student—he was maybe twenty-four. He'd transferred into the engineering program from community college after serving in the marines right out of high school. Next to his name I'd written: *old, tats, ex-marine, electrical.*

'No, that's okay,' I said. 'You're doing great.'

'I appreciate that,' he said. 'I know we already submitted our resume assignment, but, and I don't know if you've graded it yet, but I wanted to ask you something.'

'Fire away,' I said.

He didn't miss a beat. 'Should I include my community involvement in AA under Special Skills and Experiences, or no?'

'Can you explain what you mean by community involvement?' I said.

'I mean meetings,' he said. 'I'm a volunteer, I help out. I've been sober for four years. I was wondering what's your position on whether I should be honest about who I am. Will it help me or hinder me?'

Before I'd even finished my Masters in Education I knew that the academic or administrative life wasn't for me. I simply wanted to be in a classroom. Helping these younger, sharper, more ambitious kids move closer to what they wanted—it was meaningful work and I liked it. I was good at it too, taking something complicated, breaking it down into smaller more chewable parts. I showed them how coming at something, even a two-dimensional Word doc, from different angles—the side, the back, up top, so not the most direct route, maybe at the time it feeling like the long scenic route—could make that final thing better, deeper, more precise. For the most part I thought that my being in a classroom brought out the best in me too. As soon as I stepped across that threshold, I became calmer, more confident, more patient, and naturally disposed to a cheerfulness that didn't come at all naturally to me in the other parts of my life. I think this was the other reason I didn't cancel class, as that day, maybe more than most, I needed to be inside this version of myself.

What were the odds that I would be the person to discover Calvin's body? And yet, it had happened. Now I looked at this student sitting beside me with his eyes so wide. He was a grown man, really, but in that moment he was looking to me to guide him, for me to be the voice of authority and *reason*. I felt out of my depth and burdened. I could feel my best and warmest parts sluicing away.

'Who's to know?' I said. I had a hunch about what these potential employers would want to read, but I didn't want to say it. 'That's a tough one.'

The student looked at me disappointedly. I'd let him down. Still, he nodded and echoed what I'd said: 'Yeah, who's to know.'

That was when I said the thing that I'd had no intention of saying. 'You know Calvin Medina?' I said. 'The student who went missing a month ago. I was the one who found his body in the forest.'

The words escaped from me with the energy and relief of an entire bat house taking to the sky at dusk. They flew.

'Oh wow, okay,' the student said.

'It wasn't good,' I said. I shook my head. 'It was pretty

gruesome what I saw to be honest. It looked like he'd been out there for a month. Don't try and picture it. You can't. It was worse than what you're picturing. There were beetles.'

The student didn't say anything. The expression on his face was less one of disbelief than the kind I might have expected if, instead of sharing this information, I'd run my hand up the inside of his leg. In the few seconds of quiet that followed, I realised my mistake. I couldn't take it back though. It was done.

'I'm sorry I'm not much help,' I said, trying to return to the previous track, my voice wavering with panic.

The student shrugged with a visible discomfort. 'It is what it is.'

The bus home was full. I found a seat between a woman almost entirely concealed behind a wall of plastic Publix bags and a man reading a battered copy of a publication titled *Test Your Bible Knowledge*. I was lightheaded. I still hadn't eaten anything except for that single slice of toast at breakfast, and I'd drunk two coffees. On my way to the bus stop I'd stopped at a campus store and bought a pre-packaged chicken salad sandwich. It was only after I'd taken a bite that I remembered Dottie's homemade sandwiches from the day before. I'd put the sandwich back into its container and hid it inside my bag.

Though it was only in the low eighties out, the air conditioning on the bus had been cranked. When we first moved to Florida, I'd learned quickly how devoted the populace was to Air Conditioning. I soon got into the habit of carrying a sweater with me everywhere, and a pair of socks, no matter the weather, no matter if it was in the nineties out—especially if it was in the nineties out. You never knew where you might end up and how cold it might be in there.

As I was reaching into the bottom of my bag for another layer, a skinny guy got on the bus and took his place in the aisle right in my line of vision. His jeans were slipping off his arse and he was wearing a white tank top that did nothing to hide his body tattoos. His hair was slicked back. Once the bus started moving he steadied himself and reached into his satchel and removed a small bottle of cheap bourbon. I was trying not to stare, but I didn't have anywhere else to look. He must have sensed me watching, because when he'd finished drinking he looked directly at me and we made eye contact. I averted my gaze, embarrassed, but also not wanting to stir anything up. On this bus route it was best to keep a low profile. I'd recently seen a girl being pelted by a stranger with peanut butter cups while she cried, 'I'm allergic to those, allergic!' I'd seen a man tightly clutching a zip-lock bag full of cigars throw his shoulders in the direction of each new person who walked down the aisle and shout, 'What? What?' I'd seen a woman get bitten on the hand by her companion's apple-faced Chihuahua and then approach each person on the bus for their phone number so they could be a witness when she sued. I'd seen a sorority girl get verbally abused for trying to photograph another rider's court-ordered ankle bracelet. And a month ago a man had been so angry with me for not wanting to share his umbrella at the bus stop that he'd spent the whole journey cussing at me from directly across the aisle, his legs spread wide, his fists planted on his knees, while every other person on the bus pretended not to hear.

The guy with the bourbon did nothing. It was so easy not to think about how other people were really feeling. He didn't want to start anything. He was just another guy going home from work on a Friday afternoon, to some kind of family probably, maybe a partner, maybe a kid or two, the idea of it both a huge comfort, a thing to run towards, out of breath, legs aching, not wanting to miss a second, but also the opposite, a reality I understood better now, the exhaustion of it, too, how it could also be a thing to slink towards, feet dragging, breath bated.

As I put on my sweater and leaned back into my seat, I sensed a fold of pressure against my butt on the hard plastic. Dan's tissue. It had spent the day in my back pocket. I slid my hand between me and the seat to check, yes, it was still there, and the man with the Bible quiz shifted in such a way that I heard loud and clear I was taking up too much space; my shoulders were too broad and pointy.

The chicken salad sandwich I'd bought had come to $6.66 with tax. I'd commented on this to the cashier, a girl with severe acne who looked as if she should still be in high school, and she'd screwed up her face with alarm and let out a short parrot cry and said, 'No thank you no thank you.' Occasionally I still needed to be reminded that this part of Florida, while a liberal blue bubble of a university town, was also on the edge of the evangelical South. The man sitting next to me, I could sense his righteousness. It created a pressure in the air around him that made me feel accosted. The woman to my left—in her I sensed a deep weariness. She had spent the whole bus trip scooping her bags of shopping closer to her, *swish-swish*, apologising to everyone who walked past, though the bags were well out of the way. Every couple of minutes she looked down at her feet as if taking a headcount, as if her bags of frozen fish fingers, string cheese, milk, cookie dough, and toilet paper were her children and she was afraid one of them might run off.

Waiting for the bus to arrive, I'd thought about how to make it a fun afternoon for Finn. I would really work for it. Maybe

I would get out his paint set, or we would bake something, an activity that ended in enough of a mess and a disaster for me to feel like I wasn't holding back, like I was doing everything I could to be present and a good mom. Now, though, there was something about these people near me, the whole vibe of the bus really, it was a bad vibe, that made me forget all that and think about the one thing I'd spent the day avoiding thinking about, though wanted to think about the most: Jason.

On Wednesday, the day before the burn, Finn and I had attended our usual Music & Movement session at the local library. A few songs from the end, I'd left Finn with Chantelle and Wren—this was before Loren the detective insulted Chantelle over those stacking cups—while I excused myself to use the bathroom. Then I'd sought out Jason. I'd found him standing in the stacks on the other side of the children's floor.

'All going okay in there?' he'd said, nodding towards the event room.

This was where the fantasy always fractured: the hard spin of how I hoped these interactions might go versus the concrete reality of my circumstances.

'We're nearly done,' I'd said.

'Look at this.' Jason turned the book he was holding around so I could see the cover, which was an illustration of a budgerigar wearing a leotard. 'A rhythmic gymnast bird? You might think, oh there's somethin' wrong with that bird, that its wings don't work, and that's why it has taken up this particular extracurricular activity? If you did, you would be wrong.'

It was a singular enjoyment learning what specific things could push a man's buttons.

'My guess is it's a flimsy tale about *carving out your own path* while still collecting loads of admirers along the way?'

'That's dead on,' Jason said. 'You've read this one?'

This conversation wasn't what I'd come for and we didn't have time for it. I wanted to hurry things along. I wanted to say something, but all that came out was a pitiful sigh.

'Sorry,' I said. 'I don't know what that was.'

'Don't say that,' Jason said, 'sorry.' Then he reached out and hooked a finger through one of the belt loops at the front of my jeans.

I'd immediately felt drunk, struck with an inebriation so full it was destabilising. I couldn't remember how I felt the first, second, third time Dan had reached for me, though I'd been searching for the memory of it. Surely, it must have been that way then too, as for the first year of our relationship our hands would be snaking up each other's T-shirts before we could close the bedroom doors in our respective living situations, the sex hot and fast and then hot and slow, and I remember thinking, maybe I'll get to have this for the rest of my life, what luck.

With his finger still hooked into my jeans, Jason pulled me towards him. It wasn't a decisive pull, but rather a slow dragging, as if I were an anchor being winched up, the chain creaking and bumping, from some deep, murky depth, till I was standing close enough to feel the warmth and softness and hardness of his body, this other man. He smelled like supermarket deodorant—not the same brand Dan wore, but equally unfancy. Now the weight of his hands on my hips. I lightly pressed my hands to his waist, felt it give. His eyes were a mossy green and clear. I lowered my gaze to the loop of ribbon that held his library employee lanyard, then to his throat and to where his shirt was unbuttoned low enough to remind me what I would see if that shirt were removed. The first time, I'd expected to see tattoos. I'd found myself searching for them. There were none though, his skin pale and his shoulders freckled, as were his nose and cheeks, two details that made him appear younger than his forty-two years.

'Mm,' I said.

It was an involuntary utterance—the kind of sound one might make while studying a map of a foreign city and figuring out how far and in what direction the next site of interest lay. Jason exhaled in a way that suggested, though I couldn't feel it, that his pulse was racing, that he was studying me as I was studying him, and that he, too, was imagining destinations. I wanted to feel the urgency of his breath and those pictures against my own breath, my own pictures, so I closed the remaining gap between us. I'd only meant to get my heartrate going. Except when I'd reached the line that I'd believed I wouldn't cross, I saw that it wasn't enough. I'd wanted to go further and it had been so easy to simply lift my foot and step over it, that line. I circled my arms around Jason's waist, as Jason slid his hands into the back pockets of my jeans. I arched into him so I could feel the cold metal of his belt-buckle against my belly and below that the hardness of his cock. For a few seconds our bodies rose and fell together in the same hurried way, leaning into each other almost too hard, zipper to zipper, it hurting but in a good way, till the thin roar of my son and his playmates flowed out onto the library floor.

I pulled back and looked across the top of the bookshelves. The librarian who had led the Music & Movement session had opened the door to the event room. She didn't look our way, but my seeing her snapped me out of my stupor. Though I'd only been gone a few minutes, I needed to get back to that room, but I also wanted to stay right where I was, and I thought in that moment about what I'd started to believe of myself, which was that I wasn't a good person. This had become something I had identified fresh each day since the afternoon in January when Jason and I first made a connection, and was now like a creature that lived inside of me, sleeping when I slept and wriggling awake each morning as I pulled back the covers of the bed I shared with Dan, wriggling in such a way that I couldn't forget it was there, the knowledge that I was bad and maybe also undeserving.

'You round for Spring Break?' Jason said next.

I hadn't wanted to seem too eager. 'Grading papers, not much else.'

'Friday,' he said, 'come round.'

'I don't know,' I said, barely above a whisper. Then, 'I gotta go.'

I'd tried to sound resolute, but my voice had wavered. It had sounded, as clear as the snap of a flag in the wind, like I didn't want to go anywhere.

Still, I disengaged myself and turned away. I didn't look back as I returned to the event room. Though when I'd stepped away from Jason, I'd taken the hand that was on my hip and instead of coolly returning it to his side—a hand that was so dry, *from the air conditioning*, he said, the skin rivered with thin cracks, a hand that if I'd seen it on the street I wouldn't want anywhere near me, except that I did want it, I wanted it all over me—I slowly ran my thumb over his palm and all the way to the tip of his middle finger, too slowly and all that way for it to mean nothing.

Now the guy in the tank top steadied himself against a nearby bus seat, and put his bourbon back inside his satchel. As I reached up and pulled the cord for my stop, he removed a bottle of water instead. I watched as he slowly unscrewed the plastic cap and drank from it the same way he'd drunk his bourbon.

I thought, That's how a man drinks water.

I don't know. I'd said that before the other times with Jason too. The fact of it was I was already there, once again standing in his cool dimly lit hallway. I was already kissing him and he was already running his fingers in circles below the hem of my shorts, drawing them upwards while I ran my hands over his scalp, his close-cut hair both wiry and soft like a deer pelt.

As I stepped down from the bus I knew without a doubt that I would see Jason that night. Even with less than three hours sleep, even as I thought about Finn and how we would spend the afternoon together, my heart swelling as I picked up my pace turning into our street, saw our house come into view and thought about what I'd see behind the creak of the front door—Finn's face, Dan's face. I couldn't get to it fast enough, my little life. The thought that I might open the door and find it was no longer there was unbearable, too heavy to even lift, and yet I was rushing towards something else too. I could feel it. And that thing, it was flowing in a different direction.

One thing you have to do when applying for the visa that's the stepping-stone to being issued a green card is list every single address you have resided at since you were sixteen years old. At either end of this timeframe, this wasn't a tough task for me—at one end was the house I grew up in and where my parents still live, and at the other were the few apartments I'd rented with Dan. The middle section though, that was harder. There were some years I hadn't thought about in a long time, in particular the wobbly years after undergrad, and the bad years after I returned to New Zealand from Australia, the times when I was most adrift and drunk.

Lined up one after the other, these places created an itinerary of my adult life. It was a strange thing to behold. Spending so much time staring at grainy Google Earth photos of the façades of some of these houses, which was one way to confirm a long-ago address, I started to think about the bedrooms I'd kept inside them. Once I was inside those bedrooms, I began to recall the men I'd been with in them. I found I could recollect these details with a surprising clarity.

I could remember how while leaning against the wall at a party this one had brazenly snaked his hand inside the back of my jeans, and how in the early hours of the morning as we walked up my street he stepped in dog shit and had to spend five minutes scraping his shoes around in the leaves in the yard. I could remember how this one said, 'You're too young for me' over and over, right up until the point I had his dick in my hand when he finally conceded, 'Yeah okay this is fine'. I could remember the one who without ceremony unzipped his pants, leaned back on my bed and said 'Suck it' and then fell into a sneezing fit. I could remember the one whose ear gauges fell out onto my chest before he came and how vulnerable he became finally for that minute before he was done. I could remember the one who wouldn't take off his shirt or let me touch him above his pubic line. I could remember the one who confessed he had a girlfriend only once I was propped above him, his cock hard and pressing into my belly, but that he really wanted to be friends with me, *best* friends. I could remember the other ones who already had girlfriends too. I could remember which ones stopped when I asked them to stop and which ones had to be asked again or pushed away. I could also remember the few who had actually got me off, the ones who had heard the sound of my pleasure cresting and had felt my body give out as it slid down the other side, my legs twitching with it, and, in the cool weight of the silence that followed, experienced the intimacy of the moment when I came back into focus and giggled not out of embarrassment but as a kind of punctuation of gratitude.

I've never been beautiful. Not a single man has ever used that word to describe me. I'd been called *cool* most of all—a word that could feel big when coming out of the right mouth but would immediately begin to deflate—and *cute*, that minuscule word. I'd spent my whole life feeling ugly. However, I had a body that worked and so I'd used it. Then, as now, it was still an athlete's body, so not slight or lithe but lean and strong, and I knew what it could do. When I stood naked in front of a mirror in one of those bedrooms of my twenties, I would look at my face and I didn't know what I was looking at, whereas I could look at the rest of what was reflected there, and know it was mine and that it was good. Back then it had been that the faster I could take off my clothes, and the more men who could see me with my clothes off, the less I would be just a plain face with a jaw that was a little too strong, eyes that were a surprising light blue but overshadowed by the permanent dark rings beneath them. Added up, these men had made me feel that in spite of my average looks my aura was that I was fuckable, and that became self-fulfilling. This, I think, was how I'd convinced myself that the manner in which I'd spent the majority of my twenties, up till the point I met Dan, was a success.

Though Dan had also only ever used the words *cool* and *cute* to describe me, from the start it felt like he was the point I'd been moving towards. He made me feel seen. I'd spent too much time drunk and searching for the man I was meant to be with, both figuratively and literally, whereas with Dan, and not just because he was so tall, I didn't even have to look. I would turn around at a party and there he would be. The ropes that are used to guide a boat's sails and its movement—though I'm not sure which part Dan was exactly, or which part our relationship in general was. Being with him made me feel like a boat with its sails under control. Tethered. No longer flapping wildly around.

Dan proposed to me the evening of his mother's funeral. After saying goodbye to the last of our friends at the end of the wake, he grabbed a half-consumed bottle of wine and led me to the back of his parents' yard, down by the compost bin and dying vegetable garden, where we squatted beside some monstrous broccolis gone to seed and shared lukewarm swigs. Dan exhaled for the first time in months, then he turned to me and said he couldn't have survived all this without me and that he thought we should get married. 'Sure,' I said. 'I like that idea.' We might have been discussing what to order for dinner. For me, that was more romantic and meaningful than any kind of grand proposal, the kind that more than once I'd seen take place in our local park, the guy on one knee, the woman covering her face with her hands while visibly sobbing, a photographer hovering nearby, hired to capture the whole thing. Choosing to marry Dan was an easy decision, but that doesn't mean it was a light decision. We'd already decided to be together—the conversation by the vegetable garden was only a formality.

Being with Dan was a different and better kind of freedom. For a long time that had been it, and I couldn't imagine feeling any other way or wanting anything else.

Now that I'd finished washing and stacking the dinner

dishes, I gave myself time to change my mind about seeing Jason. I was already dressed in my running shorts and T-shirt. I'd put on fresh underwear. I'd got this far into leaving when I felt myself pulled back—the person I wanted to be here, and the person I needed to be with Jason, in a battle with each other.

While I was in the kitchen, Dan and Finn were playing in the living room with a booklet of reusable stickers. There were different backdrops and Finn was moving the stickers around from scene to scene so that an astronaut was flying next to a beehive in a tree next to a stingray under a toadstool next to a smiling shark. I couldn't see this exactly, but I knew from the last time Finn and I had played with it, and from what Dan was saying.

'Is the spaceship in the water? Is it swimming? With the brown bear? And the lobster?'

As I dried my hands, I stood in the doorway and watched them. Finn was trying to say 'lobster'. He was making a good go of it. I thought then, as I'd thought many times before, I hope he never loses that willingness to keep trying for something, even as he fails, to keep trying. Of course he would lose it. At some point, maybe when he hit puberty, maybe later, he would turn in on himself and become some degrees of embarrassed and ashamed and fearful, as we all do. And a man who didn't or couldn't feel those things wasn't the man I wanted him to be anyway. Though which degrees of these things were the right degrees?

I was so tired. The lack of sleep, the rollercoaster of events since the day before—it descended on me. I thought how easy it would be to go upstairs, take off my clothes, shower, put on my pyjamas, and come back downstairs and join my family.

All I had to do was lift my feet and begin walking in the right direction.

'Can you make claws like the lobster?' Dan said.

Finn was getting there.

'Like this,' Dan said. He made a snapping movement with his hands and waited for Finn to mirror him. 'That's right, well done.'

Dan and I were both readers. We never made each other mixtapes; we gave each other stories. Recently, he had showed me a short story by Barry Hannah, in which the narrator mentioned an old affair. In the shadow of his regret the man described sex with the woman who wasn't his wife as being *just arms and legs*, as being *not worth a damn*. When I'd finished reading, I'd looked at Dan and he'd repeated that part of the story about the arms and legs with a finality that made me think with a certainty I'd always had in a way, but here it was with literary emphasis, that Dan would never cheat on me.

Now Dan made a face. He leaned closer to the Finn. 'Bud, did you do poos?'

Finn didn't reply. He kept playing with his stickers.

'Bud, did you?' Dan said.

'Finn, sweetie,' I said, 'did you do poos?'

Without looking up, Finn quietly answered in a puddle of sound: 'Pooos.'

I don't know what it means that this was the thing I walked towards, and not the thing that made me walk away and out the front door and into Jason's arms.

'I'll do it,' I said.

Without thinking about it again, I edged off my trainers and walked across the living room to where Finn and Dan were sitting. 'Let's go upstairs, sweetie.'

99

Finn looked at me with such a deep melancholy. He knew he had to leave his stickers now, and that once we went upstairs the order of the night would shift, and we would begin the slow winding down to bedtime.

'Do you want me to carry you?' I said.

He stretched out his arms towards me, my almost two-year-old who was tall for his age, broad-shouldered and heavy. He had been able to walk up the stairs on his own since not long after his first birthday, but he still liked to be carried too.

'Cuddles?' he said. That lovely round word arrived like all the others, on the back of that tumbling, frothing wave, though it was no less meaningful for it.

I bent down, heaved him up. As I did, I felt a familiar twinge in my lower back. A sharp pain that was a reminder of my place here. I held Finn on my hip. He clung to me with all four limbs, fast like a koala. In that way, as we'd done hundreds, maybe thousands of times before, we climbed the stairs together.

7.

'On closer inspection,' I said, 'the bird on the ground was a large owl. It had its wings extended towards me as if they were arms. I picked it up and sat it down on a wall. It immediately fell backwards off the wall. When I peered over the side, I saw the ground was much further down on that side than the ground where I was standing, and the owl had found a shell, squeezed its way inside, and was wearing the shell as if it were a hermit crab. It was suddenly in the company of other crabs, and it went about with them, resigned to its new life.'

'That's a good one,' Dan said.

'It's boring, other people's dreams,' I said. 'I don't know why I always tell you.'

'No, I like it,' Dan said. 'They're like messed up slices of you.'

We were heading to Perry's house for dinner. It was two days after the burn. Neither of us wanted to go, and we'd had a heated discussion about whether we had an excuse not to. Dan and Perry had ended up going out the night before, Friday night, the night I'd not gone to Jason's. I'd not heard Dan come in. I didn't want to be out and social. It had been a long day. That morning I'd had my formal interview with the police about the discovery of Calvin's body, which they were still unable to refer to as Calvin's body. It had been a brief exchange that could have taken place over the phone, and yet it had also grounded what had happened for me in a new uncomfortable reality. I'd spent the remainder of the day in a haze, both tired and anxious, unsure where to sit or stand, spinning, spinning inside of myself. Perry had asked us to this dinner weeks ago though, and we'd already booked in Amber to watch Finn, so in the end undoing the plan was just as troublesome as showing up.

'You're making fun of me,' I said to Dan now. The truth was, I was telling him about this dream because I couldn't think of anything else to say.

'You know I don't dream,' Dan said. 'You know I find it interesting.'

Perry lived on the northwest side of our neighbourhood, close enough that we didn't have to drive, which meant we could both drink. I'd decided that night I would be drinking with abandon. Dan and I were both dressed in jeans and T-shirts. Dan was wearing his best Nikes and I was wearing my least-scuffed sandals. This was us dressed up these days. I'd also put on makeup and my hair was out, though I was already regretting this choice.

'I should've brought a hair tie,' I said, pulling my hair back into a ponytail in my hand. 'It's making me hot. My hair, my neck.'

Dan reached out and placed his hand on my neck underneath where I'd let my hair fall. Something shot through me—Dan's hand, my neck. It made me think of another hand there.

'What happened next in the dream?' Dan said.

I thought he was only asking this question because he, too, couldn't think of anything else to say.

'Calvin showed up,' I said.

'Oh?' Dan said. He removed his hand.

'I think I woke up after that.'

'I thought I felt you thrashing about.'

That night and the first night after the burn, Calvin had been present in my dreams as much as my own consciousness. Both nights, my dreamscape opened with a blurry version of what I'd seen in the forest, as if my brain was trying to censor it for me. Then the Calvin I remembered from my classroom would appear by my side, and we would look at his corpse together. I would apologise for crying about it, and Calvin would say, 'No, it's fine, everyone has feelings, it's good to both express and name your feelings', and we would hold hands like a mother and son. I would think, I wonder if Finn will still hold my hand this way when he's twenty, probably not, and I would be momentarily annoyed at my boy who wasn't there, though I knew instinctively that he was safe, though it was a fragile instinct with a hard buzz of worry about it. What did Calvin and I do in these dreams after this? Mostly more free association nonsense, like the owl in the crab shell, which would get wilder and more disturbing as the night wore on, till my brain eventually expelled me and I woke at a dark heavy hour, my body prickling, thick with goosebumps, as if I'd received the fright of my life.

'I hope I didn't wake you,' I said to Dan.

'Not really,' he said, a man who would forever sleep deep and undisturbed, a kind of sleep I could only wish for. 'Just a bit.'

We saw Perry before we saw his house. He was standing in the middle of the street, beer in hand, looking up into the live oak that stood directly opposite his front path. It was growing half through the sidewalk, half through the road. As we drew closer, Perry looked in our direction and raised his can in greeting.

'Sally's out,' he said.

'Sally?' I said.

'My superstar layer,' he said. 'She thinks she's roosting here tonight.'

He pointed to one of the thick horizontal branches a couple of rungs up. I squinted. There she was, a handsome tawny-coloured hen, sitting smug.

'I didn't know you had hens,' I said.

'I thought y'all called them "chooks",' Perry said.

'Sometimes,' I said.

'Perry has four hens, one rooster,' Dan said.

It turned out that Perry had had the hens for nearly a year. Not knowing this made me feel as if I'd been living on a different planet. Where had I been?

'I'm surprised she could get that high up,' I said, nodding at Sally.

'The build of a weightlifter, the lift of a ballerina,' Perry said. He shrugged. 'She'll be all right. I'm just praying she ain't laying tonight.'

It took till I was standing in Perry's hallway to figure what he meant. It was easily a one-storey drop to the road below from where Sally was perched. If she was laying, it wasn't good for Perry, but someone, a raccoon or an opossum probably, would be getting a free breakfast. The thought of this oddly cheered me—the neat circle of suburban Florida life.

'Can you check my eye again?' Dan said, as soon as I closed the front door.

'We're in here,' Perry said, from the other end of the hallway. He was standing in the doorway that opened into the dining-living room.

'Give us a second,' Dan said.

'Right now?' I said. Dan had periodically asked me to check his eye since Thursday night. 'Why didn't you ask before we left home?'

'I forgot,' he said.

'I don't know why you won't see a doctor,' I said. 'I also don't know why you're still wearing your contact lenses. That seems really dumb.'

'I told you the contacts make it feel better.'

'So, what am I looking for?'

'I don't know,' he said. 'Anything.'

He bent over so his head was on my level and, in what had become our most intimate interaction for a while, this awkward pose of the last two days, and though I already knew what I would find, which was nothing, Dan held open his eyelid and waited for me to lean into him and look.

When Americans ask me to tell them what New Zealand is like, they often add: 'Is it so beautiful?' So I am forced to reply: 'Yes, it's so beautiful'. The next thing I say is that it's also small, one sprawling small town, really. The whole two degrees of separation thing, I say, it's mostly true. You would be hard pressed to meet someone who doesn't know someone you also know. The thing about where we lived in Florida was that, despite the large size of the university, our city was a proper small town, made smaller by the fact that almost everyone we knew lived in this neighbourhood or one neighbourhood over. So, I shouldn't have been surprised to see Jason enter the room behind Perry's roommate Kat.

On seeing Kat and Jason arrive one after the other from the direction of what I imagined was Kat's bedroom, I felt myself swell with jealousy. Perry's girlfriend Lucy had handed me a drink as soon as Dan and I entered the room, and as I watched Jason move about, clearly as stunned to see me as I was to see him, I found myself drinking in hot little sips. He was barefoot and wearing his black cut-offs with a long-sleeved pearl-snap shirt that was buttoned to the top. He wasn't tall—a bit taller than me, nowhere near as tall as Dan. Whenever I saw him, I couldn't help but do this—mentally compare the two of them, as if this was a pig picking and my next move would be to get out my tape measure and ask Jason to raise his arms so I could measure his circumference. And now here they were, standing side by side. By the time I stepped out in front of it and introduced Jason to Dan as I knew him—a librarian who Finn and I sometimes saw at Music & Movement—my glass was almost drained. Dan responded to the introduction with a handshake and a *That's cool*, which betrayed nothing. Though later I would remember how fast he'd finished his first drink, too, and how I'd absently thought, Dan seems thirsty, and, I hope he doesn't get too wasted.

Despite my moving around the table in a monumentally noncommittal dance, Jason ended up sitting to my left, Dan to my right, the three of us sharing a bench seat. I allowed myself one furtive glance at Jason's profile. He had the face of a man who has never been very good looking nor very unattractive either, but a face that at some point in recent years, and with some weathering and resignation, had started to make sense.

He wasn't as good looking as Dan, but his face, it made me ache in a different way. Those freckles too—concentrated on his nose and becoming more diluted as they spread onto the ledge of his cheeks. This feature did something to me, as did his Alabama accent.

Out of the corner of my eye I watched as he drew a wobbly circle with his index finger clockwise around the circumference of his dinner plate. I wondered if he was stoned. The fact of him being a stoner wasn't something I'd registered till I'd been inside his house the first time and during the forty-five minutes we were in each other's company had watched him light up twice. The keenness of his actions, they weren't of a person getting baked at a party, but the reflex of a man for whom weed was like water—a necessary part of his being. He drew another circle now, counterclockwise this time.

Perry had set the table with a tablecloth and lit candles. He'd prepared three different proteins (shrimp, carnitas, chicken) and made tortillas from scratch. I couldn't think of another time in all the years we had been friends that he had spent this much effort preparing a meal. Usually, dinner at Perry's meant a cookout, hotdogs-in-buns kind of affair. He was trying something on. There were eight of us sitting around the table, which wasn't really big enough for so many guests, so we were all sitting shoulder to shoulder. Jason had done his best to position himself as far down the bench seat as was practicable, while I was doing my best to sit as close to Dan as was humanly possible without sitting in his lap. Even so, the air between Jason and me was only a hand's width.

Lucy kept the drinks coming, so that while my mind was spinning with all the ways this could come undone, the rest of the table quickly became jolly and familiar. I got drunk fast too.

I found it impossible to concentrate on what anyone was talking about. I was focusing a lot of attention on eating my dinner without making a mess, and I was watching Kat. I didn't know what she did, didn't want to know, though she had the large nervous motions of a theatre type. I was also hyperaware of the arms and legs on the bench seat. There were Dan's arms and legs, my right side pressed against his left side, as was normal and expected, but my left side—it was as if I'd forgotten how to use that share of my body. I didn't know where to put my hand, or how to angle that foot. I was afraid of accidentally touching Jason and reacting wrong—too big or too small. I felt myself bottoming out.

For the longest time, during the second half of my pregnancy and after Finn's birth, I didn't even think about sex. Then one day it finally popped back into my head—round and crisp and shiny, like an apple plucked fresh from beneath the mister in the supermarket. Though Jason had been working at the library for as long as Finn and I had been going there, suddenly there he was too. One afternoon in January after a Music & Movement session, Finn marched away from me, picked up a colouring sheet from the trolley next to the issuing desk, and took a seat at one of the activity tables. I watched this unfold with amusement. Jason was watching too, and when Finn sat down he took out a plastic container from behind the desk where he was sitting and scooped up a handful of crayon nubs for me to give to Finn. As he emptied the crayons into my hands, his hands separating like the bucket of a digger depositing a load of gravel, I raised mine too abruptly, so for a moment our hands were cupped together. My hands, Jason's hands. We both lingered.

It was something. It still destabilises me to remember it even now. And this, I think, is why: when I finally closed my fingers around those waxy crayon nubs, I found that a door in the long corridor of my marriage, a door that I knew must exist but which I'd never bothered to search for, in fact had not wanted to search for in the eight years I'd been with Dan, had inched open a crack, with a whistle of cool air and a thin line of light.

I wasn't sure that door would ever properly close again.

Now, sitting on that bench seat, my peripheral vision pressed on by the figures of these two men, I thought, I'm the world's unluckiest woman.

Then I thought, No, I deserve this.

'So, what's the latest on that dude that went missing?' Lucy said. Like Jason, she was from Alabama, though her accent generally wasn't a very Southern one, except for when she was drinking, at which point it started to roll through like heavy ropes of seaweed washing in with the Gulf tide. 'They found him in the forest? That was the dude, the one they found?'

I tuned in. As far as I knew, only Dan and Perry were aware that I'd been in the group that had discovered Calvin's body, which still hadn't been formally identified, though everyone spoke of it as if it had been decided. Judging by Lucy's question, Perry hadn't told her anything about my connection. I looked at him, and he returned my look with a guise of concern that appeared completely unrelated to me and this topic of conversation and that made me think that he was off on a different plane.

'The dead dude?' I'd said almost nothing over the course of the dinner so far, and my voice sounded raw, unsure.

'What?' Lucy said, her cheeks rosy with booze.

She was finishing a clinical psychology PhD after which she was leaving for greener pastures. She hadn't yet asked Perry if he would go with her and she likely wouldn't, according to Dan. I hadn't known about Perry's hens, but I knew this. I thought then how the dinner was probably for Lucy, a last attempt on Perry's part to show her something.

'Calvin Medina,' I said. 'That's his name. And they still haven't formally IDed the body.'

'Formally IDed?' Kat said. She sniggered.

'They're looking at a classmate or classmates. There's a story there,' Simon said. He was an adjunct teacher like me, but in the business school. 'The whole thing is just so unusual.'

'I overheard someone talking about it in Chipotle yesterday,' Lucy said. 'There were a group of them, his friends, who were involved?'

'So unusual,' Simon said.

'Unusual is a word for it,' Sam said. He was Simon's partner, and from what I could gather he worked in the county clerk's office. 'How'd he get all the way out there, that's what I can't make sense of?'

'I heard it was only an accident though,' Kat said.

'Chance would be a fine thing,' Jason said.

Jason had also spoken infrequently so far that evening. Dan could happily sit through a dinner party and not say a single thing except, 'Can you please pass the hot sauce?' That was who he was. I didn't know Jason well, but I knew he liked to talk, that that was who he was. I liked hearing him speak now, for this simple fact, and also because I was trying to trawl his words and tone for clues to where we were at. I hadn't shown up at his house the night before as planned. Was it nothing to him or was he hurt? Had he been watching the clock? I wanted to believe he'd waited, and I wanted to feel the weight of every one of those minutes. The picture of him waiting was intoxicating to me. It made me want to touch him, to reach across and slip my hand beneath the frayed denim of his cut-offs and slide it as far up his leg as I could. I wanted to let him know that I'd wanted to go, that even though I hadn't, I'd wanted to.

'Is it bad to say that's disappointing?' Simon said. 'It's still curious, but I was hoping for something juicier.'

'Yeah, but what kind of accident lands you in the middle of the forest?' Kat said. 'And no one knowing where you are for, what, like a month?'

'I keep thinking about turkey vultures,' Dan said.

All sets of eyes at the table turned on Dan, surprised, I believe, to hear him speak. Though I didn't say it at the time, this was also something I'd thought about: the scavenger birds circling, and why they hadn't acted like a flare to Calvin's body. Or was this because they were always circling above something, and this was just Florida?

'Those student athletes,' Jason said, ignoring Dan's comment, 'they have no good outlets for all the pressure.' He said this as if speaking from personal experience.

'I had a running back almost in tears in my office the other day,' Simon said.

'Maybe he was struck by lightning,' Sam said.

'Cottonmouth bite,' Kat said.

'Pressure from all sides too,' Simon said. 'Team, school, home, not to mention what they put on themselves.'

'Hopes and dreams,' Jason said.

'Hopes and dreams,' I said.

When I consider this evening and the days that were to follow and how they unfolded, those three words sit loudly in my heart, the sound and shape and meaning of them. It was only after I'd said them and I'd seen Dan turn to me, first, and

Jason move uncomfortably, second, that I realised I'd repeated what Jason had said out loud and not just in my head. I'd only wanted to feel those words in my mouth because they had so recently been in Jason's mouth. It was a reflex borne from desire and from wanting to reduce the space between me and my lover. Yet, they were three words with an unmistakable weight which made me acknowledge for the first time that what I'd done with Jason, how I felt about him and how it had disturbed my life, wasn't frivolous.

'You would think someone would know where he was,' Lucy said.

A silence settled on the room. It wasn't connected to what I'd said, or even that everyone was taking a moment to think about Calvin, but rather more a general dragging of boredom at this topic of conversation. When Calvin had first been reported missing, I'd noticed that in the space of a few days, the size of the font and the position of the headline relating to his case had shrunk and dropped, like a balloon animal deflating. The same was happening again, from the first headline immediately following the discovery of his body, to the last time I'd refreshed the news that afternoon.

Jason was the one to break the brief quiet. 'Did anyone live here when the serial killer, the slasher or whatever he went by, was workin'?'

'Working?' Dan said with an unfamiliar meanness.

'You know what I'm sayin' here,' Jason said. 'You know what I'm sayin'.'

Dan bristled—Dan, my lowkey, people-pleaser husband, who wasn't really bothered by anyone, who embodied the expression 'water off a duck's back' to the point where it often infuriated me.

'Was it in the Nineties?' Jason said.

The answer to Jason's question was that no one had been living here. We'd all arrived from other cities, states, countries, and all within the last decade. The fact that there had been a serial killer in this town working not far from where we were eating and drinking now was removed from our experience of this city, our experience of life anywhere. We'd been blissfully untouched.

'He decapitated them you know,' Lucy said.

'Oh right, yeah,' Kat said, 'is he the one who put the heads up, like, on a shelf?'

'I did not know that,' Lucy said, sadly.

'I didn't know that either,' Simon said.

'I did,' Sam said.

'He did it,' Jason said, 'so the women, in death, would have no choice but to look down at themselves.'

'Eww,' Kat said.

'So their heads had to look at where they'd previously been,' Lucy said.

The table fell quiet again. If anyone else was like me they were picturing their own severed head up there on a dusty IKEA shelf, surrounded by college textbooks, an incense holder, bong and lighter, a jar of change, a postcard from the Dali Museum in St Pete, the crappy stuff of student accommodation, eyes open and lips slightly parted, with a prime view of their own naked, head-free body down there on the floor, propped up as it was against the base of the couch, legs spread, arms hanging dead.

As I was thinking this, I saw Kat reach for Jason. She wanted him to pass her the bowl of fresh chili, her fingers pressed gently to his forearm where it rested on the tabletop. I noticed how she lingered, it was a touch of familiarity, and Jason didn't immediately pull back.

One afternoon at the library, in the stretch between when my hands and Jason's hands were cupped together and the first time at Jason's house, he had appeared beside me at the board books shelf. I was searching for books to check out for Finn, who was sitting at my feet. As I let my fingers hover over the fat cardboard spines and hunted for something to say, Jason spoke. 'Your arms,' he said, 'they're beautiful.' Then I watched as he sketched a line with his eyes from my hand all the way up my arm to where it disappeared into the sleeve of my T-shirt. At the time, this interaction had been overwhelming. Since then, though, I'd heard Jason use the word beautiful to describe many things, including one of his more boring-looking house plants, his bicycle, his leather belt, my leather belt, his collection of sharks' teeth, a friend's tattoo that he had a picture of on his phone, the broken chandelier in his hallway, a cobweb on his porch, a can of beer he was drinking once, a water stain on his bedroom ceiling that looked a bit like a squid.

'Calvin Medina,' I said, 'the student we were just talking about. I was the one who found him.'

As with the first time I'd said this, to my student the afternoon before, the words came out in a rush. There was no wild bat energy this evening though. It didn't feel as good.

'The turkey vultures weren't circling anymore, because they were done with him,' I said. I was swinging out of control. 'It was worse than what you're picturing. Much, much worse. You could fit what was left of him into a bucket, just fold and scrape and pour it all in.'

'I do not want to see that,' Lucy said.

'That does not sit well in my stomach,' Simon said.

'I'm not talking about some giant tin drum,' I said. 'I'm talking about a regular garden pail, like you might use for your compost, for feeding the pigs.'

Several things happened next. First, I looked in Perry's direction and saw him shaking his head, but not in sympathy, in something else. I saw that Lucy had begun trying to suppress a bad welling up of laughter. I saw Jason withdraw his arm from Kat and fold it into his lap. Lastly, I saw Dan reach up and lightly tap on his eyelid in a way I associated with him wanting to rub his eye while wearing contact lenses, and when he was done with that, reach across the table and pick up his glass of water and drain it in one long gulp.

It was often pretty clear, really, the shape of the power in a relationship. Who leaned toward whom, who looked to whom for approval, the wanting of those things radiating out from that person like contour lines on a map. The reverse of those things—that was also often right there if you bothered to look.

A couple of the dinner guests wanted details. They wanted me to explain how I'd been in a position to find Calvin. Then they wanted to know more about prescribed burns. Then they wanted to go back to Calvin and see what else I knew about the circumstances of his death. Neither Jason nor Dan spoke.

'I was in a class with a woman who attacked her boyfriend with a hammer,' Lucy said.

The bench seat was suddenly very hard and cold beneath me.

'Did you say hammer?' Perry said.

'That can't have worked out well,' Simon said.

'A hammer?' Perry said, in a disbelief that was bordering on anger.

'It was during my honours year,' Lucy said. 'She took the

hammer with her in her handbag to the bar, and when her boyfriend went to the bathroom she followed him inside.'

'No way,' Perry said.

'Into the men's toilet,' Lucy said.

'Oof,' Sam said.

'Which end did she use?' Kat said.

I suddenly felt too warm, like I needed to shed a layer, but also like I was burning with the pressure of being pushed in on both sides by Dan and Jason, neither of whom had reached for me or given me any signs of comfort after what I'd said. I became gripped by a feeling of immense dread.

'I remember her handbag,' Lucy said. 'It was nice, a bona fide leather handbag, expensive.' She paused to demonstrate with her hands the size and shape of the bag. 'Faux snakeskin. Maybe a strange handbag for a student to have.'

'I imagine she'd use the hammer end,' Simon said.

'Which end is worse?' Kat said.

'The end with the hooks,' Dan said. 'You still got the weight, but it's sharp too.'

I remembered an incident from my swimming years, when a kid I knew climbed into the narrow overflow section of the training pool, between the drain and the pool deck, and how he had got stuck in there, his skull pushed in from both sides. He had nearly drowned.

'How did she carry her laptop and stuff, though?' I asked now. It was a weird thing to bring up, but it was all I could think of, and I wanted to bring myself back into the conversation, from which I felt I'd both expelled myself and been expelled.

'What do you mean?' Kat said.

I was hemmed in and worried. I also suddenly, desperately, needed to see Finn.

'I think she carried a tote bag too?' Lucy said.

'And you knew this person?' Dan said.

'We were friends,' Lucy said.

'Handbag, tote, hammer,' Kat said, as she mimed putting first one bag on, then another, then picking up a hammer. 'Like, holy shit.' She started to laugh.

I turned on the bench seat so I was angled towards Dan. I placed my hand on his shoulder, so he knew without my saying that I needed him to move.

'Did she go to jail?' Kat said.

'She did,' Lucy said.

'Did she finish her degree?' Simon said.

'That I do not know,' Lucy said.

It probably looked like I was getting up to use the bathroom. Except once I'd left the room, I continued down the hallway, opened the front door and screen door, walked across Perry's porch and down his front steps and out into the street. I breathed deeply and looked up into Perry's live oak. I could see only branches, darkness.

'Sally,' I said, 'I gotta check on my boy.'

I began walking towards home. Before I reached the first intersection, I realised I did in fact need to pee. I broke into a run. By the time I'd reached our house I was out of breath and had worked myself into a state. On my way, I'd passed some younger people heading out. One guy called out to my back, 'Never give up!' I must have looked like I was being pursued.

I'd left my phone and keys in my bag at Perry's and thought knocking on the front door might be a strange thing to do, so I unlatched the garden gate and approached the house from across the yard. We didn't have curtains on that side. The neighbour's lights were off, but I could still faintly see the shape of her living room. Our side was all lit up. Amber was sitting on the couch intensely studying her laptop, giant headphones on, her hands twisting one of her braids. It wasn't a good feeling being able to see her like that while I knew she couldn't see me. I was worried I would see something I shouldn't. I was also not so drunk that I didn't think about how much of a fright I could give her if I suddenly slid open the door and emerged unexpectedly from the darkness. I wasn't even sure that the sliding door was unlocked. Now that I could see our house and Amber, I was less concerned about Finn. I knew what I would find if I went upstairs. I'd acted strangely, rashly. I didn't know if I could make it all the way back to Perry's without first peeing though—now that became the more pressing need. So I went back through the gate, up our front steps, and knocked on the front door after all. Amber didn't answer. She was wearing those headphones. I knocked harder and longer till she eventually let me in. She looked dazed. One of her braids had been picked undone into a crinkled fan of blonde.

'I forgot my keys,' I said, by way of explanation.

'Is everything okay?' she said, as she stepped aside.

'Just a pitstop.' I sounded drunk.

I didn't wait around to say anything else to Amber—I headed directly upstairs. As I climbed, the sound of Finn's white-noise machine grew louder, and I could feel my heartrate slowing with it. *Glub-glub, glub-glub.* First, I used the bathroom. I didn't turn on the lights. I could see the towel rack still propped up against the wall, where I'd left it on Thursday night. It pained me, that sight, made a lump form in the back of my throat. I crept into Finn's room next, giving my eyes time to adjust to the dark. His white-noise machine was shaped like an owl. It also doubled as a nightlight that projected a spray of stars and a moon onto the ceiling. The original one had broken after being dropped on the hard tile of the bathroom floor and for the two nights we'd had to survive before its replacement arrived, we'd filled Finn's bedroom with fans, a different kind of white noise, which Finn hadn't liked. He'd stood in his crib and scanned his room with a crushed and quizzical look that I recognised as a primitive form of grief.

Now I could hear him breathing. His head was at the opposite end of his crib to his pillow. He was almost too big for the crib now. Head to toes he almost touched either end, but he would be happy in there for a while longer. It was his nest. He was sleeping on his side, curled up. That was all I wanted to see. I reached down, placed my hand flat on his back so I could feel his breath rise and fall, once, twice, three times, then I left.

'See you soon,' I called out to Amber as I crossed the living room.

I moved quickly. I'd been gone from Perry's too long. I didn't want to explain myself to anyone, so this time I ran from the start. Though I was tired, the alcohol was still there inside me and it helped me along. I could hear myself breathing raggedy, and the wet slap of my sandals on the slick asphalt. I was running through a suburban neighbourhood, but under that tunnel of live oak branches and a few dim and flickering streetlights, I felt covered as if I were in a forest.

A few years after the summer in my childhood when the forest was burned, I was running through the part that had survived with my brother Gerard. I'd been playing out there with a friend, and I'd left my watch beside a pond where we'd been fishing for eels. The watch, a Casio with a black leather strap, was a gift from my parents on my ninth birthday. Gerard knew the fastest route to the pond from where my mother was waiting on the road beside our car, so he led the way. I followed behind, keeping pace as we ran in and out of the pines, not sticking to any kind of path. We reached the pond and retrieved the watch, which was sitting on a mound of pine needles exactly where I'd left it. The sun was going down.

On the way back to the car, Gerard and I got turned around. I watched him change tack once, twice. I heard him mutter 'No, no, no', as he glanced behind him to make sure I was still there. Only a few months before, the skeletal remains of a young woman had been found in the same forest. She'd been missing for three years, and her body had been found not exactly where we were lost now, but amongst these trees and in *our community*. I understood little of what had happened, of the crime, but hearing the name of our town in the news was both exciting and terrifying, and that feeling had stuck with me. Out there during the day with my friend, it had been far from my thoughts, but now as the sun was starting to drop, and with Gerard clearly panicking too, it filled me with worry. I thought we might never escape. When we eventually emerged fifty yards down the road from where our mother was parked, I was quietly sobbing. As we walked along the verge towards our waving and smiling mother, Gerard bent sideways and vomited into the ditch. When he was done he looked at me and wiped his hand across his mouth. 'That was scary,' he said. I can't think of another time in our lives where he presented himself so wholly to me. It filled me with fear and joy at once. 'Yeah, it was,' I said. He nodded, and we never spoke of it again.

The two sides of this memory—the initial fear of being lost in the forest with the *skeletal remains*, and the feeling of my brother giving so much of himself to me—caught me out. I needed to call him, my brother. And it made me think that there was some truth in the shared experience of fear followed by the relief of coming out the other side together, because from that day on it seemed like Gerard took me more seriously, that my presence bugged him less. I was afraid of so much, but what about Dan? What did he fear? It occurred to me with some surprise that I didn't know. If Dan's life depended on me knowing the answer to that question, I couldn't have said with any kind of certainty.

I was a couple of blocks from Perry's house with this thought spinning in my head when I tripped on a raised ridge of sidewalk, pushed up by the roots of a nearby tree, which I'd not been able to fully see by the streetlight. Initially, I skipped a couple of steps, and I thought I had caught myself, but then my foot hit something slippery, a leaf probably, wet and slick from a recent rain shower, and both my legs shot out behind me, and I fell to my knees and my hands.

'Whoops,' I said, loudly and to no one.

I stood quickly and clapped my hands together, looked around. The street was quiet. No one had seen. I brushed my knees free of the leaves and gunk that I could feel there. My jeans were wet, and my hands gritty.

'That was dumb,' I said, again to no one.

As soon as I opened Perry's front door I saw Dan standing in the hallway with his phone to his ear. When he saw me, his face fell with relief and also screwed up in frustration.

'Where were you?' he said.

I quietly closed the door behind me. 'I needed some air.'

Dan's mind looked like it was spinning. He scowled. 'I was trying to call you. I thought something terrible had happened.'

Was this what Dan feared? That I would vanish? Or that I would vanish and then reappear like this?

'What could've happened?' I said.

'You've been gone for half an hour. I got freaked out,' he said. He dabbed at his eye in a way that on reflection made it clear that it was bothering him and that all the booze wasn't enough to completely numb what was progressing in there. I didn't register this at the time though. He was still scowling at me. 'I think I must be quite drunk. What's that on your hands?'

My hands were dark with filth and speckled red with scratches. At the sight of those scrapes, a faint heat bloomed.

'I fell over,' I said.

'Your knees,' Dan said.

'I'm going to use the bathroom,' I said.

'Hey,' Dan said, and reached for me, took me by the arm. 'Hey, hey.'

'What?' I said, my voice betraying more emotion than I'd intended.

'I love you, eh?' he said.

'Yep,' I said.

It wasn't the right response. I know that. But Dan had such an immensely worried look on his face, and I didn't want to hear it. Not there and not then. His tenderness and concern embarrassed me.

When I'd cleaned myself up, I returned to the dining space. Everyone was done eating. Kat, Lucy, and Simon had migrated to the couches. Sam was helping Perry clear the table. Jason was hovering. When he saw me he made a face. I couldn't make out what it meant. My stomach cartwheeled, a spin of joy and want, but I also sensed myself being pulled down and away. It was the first time I'd really felt that in relation to Jason—a bad sinking feeling. The first whisper of rejection.

'How's it going?' I said. It was a nothing thing to say.

'Good,' he said. A nothing reply.

Dan was right behind me, so I gave Jason a wide berth and helped Perry and Sam finish cleaning up. Dan stood with us in the kitchen for a bit before disappearing into the living room with a fresh beer. After he left, Jason arrived barefoot in the kitchen with two bowls, one with the last of the chili, the other with a couple of cilantro stalks. After looking around dumbly for a moment, he placed them on to the counter in an empty corner by the stove. It irritated me to see him floating like that, like an incompetent, and I also sensed the beginnings of a new feeling toward him—a cringe. And yet I still didn't want him to go. I threw him a look, though the problem was I didn't know what I wanted to say with that look.

'Get yourself another beer,' Perry said to Jason. 'There's heaps in there.'

'I appreciate it,' Jason said. 'Thank you.'

He reached into the fridge and withdrew a can. As he opened it, he caught my eye. It seemed clear he didn't know what he wanted to say either. I remember thinking, My life isn't a Muriel Spark novel, there's no way to flash forward and find out if I make it out of the housefire alive. I imagine that what Jason saw on my face was panic and resignation.

'Thanks for this,' I said to Perry when only the two of us remained in the kitchen. I was wiping down the counter while Perry scraped the leftover meat into a bowl, including just three curves of shrimp.

'Course,' he said, 'thank you for coming. I know it's been a strange few days for y'all.'

123

'Are you and Lucy okay?'

'It's been fun while it lasted,' was all Perry said.

'Oh,' I said. 'I'm sorry.'

Perry finished drying his hands. 'Do you want to say hi to the rest of my hens?'

It seemed like a weird thing to do so late at night, but I obliged. We went out via the back door. I could see the henhouse by the light in the kitchen. It was a child's playhouse the shape of a miniature villa, with the yard and mini picket fence covered over with wire netting.

'It's to keep things out rather than keep the hens in,' Perry said.

'What kind of things?' I said.

'Dogs, cats, raccoons, opossums, skunks, owls, hawks, snakes.'

'That's a lot of potential threats.'

'They're sleeping.'

'It is night time.'

'I love my hens,' Perry said. He sighed a deep sigh of the drunk and melancholy and began swaddling his hands in his T-shirt, a ratty old South Carolina football number. On his bottom half he was wearing basketball shorts. I thought how Dan and I in our jeans and T-shirts had gotten too dressed up for dinner. Everyone else was wearing cut-offs or what looked like swim shorts, old T-shirts and tank tops, as if they'd all arrived from the beach or working out. Arms out, legs out.

'You sure you're okay?' I said.

'I wanted to see if you were okay,' Perry said, turning to face me.

'Who me?'

'I've been thinking.' He dropped his hands free of his T-shirt.

'We're fine,' I said.

'Okay,' Perry said, unconvinced. 'Dan's my best friend.' He nodded his head back towards the house. 'I just want to see y'all happy. That's all.'

I got the feeling that wasn't all. I don't think a single friend in New Zealand had ever taken me aside in this way for a talk. I wondered next how much of our life Dan shared with Perry—how much of the bad, how little of the good.

'I tell them what to do but they don't listen,' Perry said.

I understood that he was back to speaking about his hens.

'Thanks for saying that,' I said.

'I, no—' Perry said. He wanted to say something else.

'What?' I said.

'I don't know what's going on there. It's not really my business.' He jerked his head back toward the house. I could just make out the way he squinted at me. It was an interrogative squint.

I didn't say anything. We held eye contact.

'What do you mean?' I said, finally.

'I like Jason,' he said. 'And just so you know, I didn't invite him.'

I could feel my heart beating thick and dry in my throat. Every drink I'd consumed that night evaporated out of my system. I felt as sober as a concrete slab.

'I like you more,' Perry said. He scratched at his face absently as he looked at the ground. The grass was scrappy out there, high and wild in places, the earth bald in others. Then he looked up, held my gaze, resolute. 'I like Dan most of all.'

I was ready to leave. I wanted to be home and in my bed, on the ridge of falling asleep, the sound of Finn's white-noise machine pulsing around me in the darkness. I also wanted to be with my husband. It was like Perry had conjured him, not just Dan, the man I lived with and argued with, but the figure of my husband as the man I had agreed to marry beside a copse of dead broccoli the evening of his mother's wake. The ideal of him.

'Y'all are good together, I think,' Perry added.

I couldn't find a single thing to say. Suddenly, we were walking back across the yard to the house. As we walked, I saw Jason lit up and framed by the kitchen window.

Though I already knew what he would say, I asked Perry, 'Does Dan know?'

'Yes,' he said.

And just like that we were back inside the house. I avoided the kitchen and followed Perry back into the living room, and I felt like I was an inch outside myself, like a poorly registered screen print. At one end, the room was discussing what Paul Reubens was doing now, and at the other, which beaches in Florida you could legally drive on. Dan turned around in his seat to face me. He looked pale. He needed to get more sun, spend more time outdoors. Maybe that was something we could do together. He also needed to shave. It had taken me till now to see how the stubble he usually kept to a shadow was bordering on a full-blown beard. It wasn't a good beard. It was long in parts and patchy in others, and his moustache was curling over his top lip and into his mouth. His eyes, the deep stunning sea blue of them—I held them as I walked across the room and sat down on the arm of his chair.

'You okay?' he said. His tone betrayed so little that I allowed myself to think he didn't guess what Perry and I had been talking about.

'Almost ready to go home, I think.'

'Let me finish this,' he said. He skulled the last of his beer.

I could hardly look anyone in the eye as we said goodbye.

I tried to make out like I was tired, and I did feel tired, so very tired. I didn't allow myself a last glance at Jason before we left. Instead, I stared at my phone, seeing for the first time the missed calls from Dan the thirty minutes that I'd been gone, and one message that read: *Are you still here?*

As we passed under Perry's live oak I squinted up into the darkness. I still couldn't see Sally, only the thick twist of branches faintly outlined by the streetlight down the way. I instinctively thought of Calvin, and I wondered how much of his death he'd had to endure alone. If he had been left out there by someone, conscious or unconscious, what had he heard, what rustling of leaves and grass, which animals making noises in the night? I tried to think back to the previous month. Had the nights still been cold? They probably had been.

On the two mornings since the burn, I'd woken from my broken sleep with a start and gone straight to Finn's room, heart pounding. When I found him happily sitting in his crib burbling away to his ragdoll elephant, I didn't immediately think about what I'd dreamed or how Calvin had been there. It was only as the day drew on that I remembered those adventures Calvin and I went on at night, and it made me feel extraordinarily sad, as if I'd known that boy, my student, much better than I had in reality. In a couple of days, Calvin had become a permanent fixture of my psyche. He had taken up residence in the space directly behind my eyes, so everything was now shadowed by his presence.

I was still looking into the live oak. Dan was beside me, standing close.

'She'll be okay,' he said. 'She'll be tucked away somewhere.'

Then before I could respond he reached out and took my hand.

The thing that I'd been rushing toward, I knew then that it wasn't Jason. I'd become so consumed by him, by thoughts of his body and my body. Dan and I walked in silence down the dark, damp streets of our neighbourhood. I couldn't remember the last time we'd held hands, done this thing that should have brought me a big comfort but didn't. I thought how I'd been waiting for something to happen to shake Dan and me out of this strange unhappy place. I'd hoped it would be something good that would bring us together, a mutual joy, but now I wondered if in fact what we had needed was a disaster. And if that was the case, was this it? Would this do?

Dan held my hand till we reached the corner of our block. Then he let it drop.

'*So the women, in death.*' He said this half a register lower than usual, in a cruel imitation of an Alabama drawl and vibrating with an unfamiliar violence. Then he moved ahead of me, put a step between us.

'What?' I said.

'That guy, he looks like a fucking *cool* youth pastor.'

8.

I'd thought it was an unspoken agreement between Dan and me that I wouldn't be taking Finn to Music & Movement again. Unspoken because, although it was now Wednesday, in the days since Perry's dinner we still hadn't got close to discussing what we both knew the other knew. I couldn't tell you anything detailed about how those days had passed except that Dan had gone to work, I'd taken care of Finn, grading papers when he napped, and that when the three of us were under the same roof come dinnertime the mood wasn't tense, but polite, which was much worse. I'd watched people on TV who'd had affairs say how much they loved their partner despite what their actions might suggest, and I'd not been able to fathom it. Before I met Dan, sex had always meant the possibility of partnership, a future, love. Now that I had that future, and until the last few days believed I still had that love, I thought sex with someone else would mean something different, something less. Did Dan still love me? I didn't know. I hadn't offered to sleep on the couch, hadn't offered anything. The wide, polite space between us—I thought it might be Dan figuring out what he wanted to say, and so I'd decided the best thing I could offer him was that space to think.

Then on Wednesday morning, before he left for work, Dan asked if I would be taking Finn to Music & Movement.

'No, definitely not,' I said, colouring in the outline of everything we hadn't spoken about directly.

'You should,' he said.

I didn't know what I was meant to say next.

'Take him,' he said.

This wasn't a suggestion, but a cool and calm order. I didn't recognise the timbre of Dan's voice. It was like I was standing across the kitchen from a complete stranger. I thought then, with a terrifying certainty, He's going to leave me.

Finn and I left the house with more than enough time. As we dawdled through the neighbourhood, I spotted Loren and her son, Alexander. I followed them—we had time to kill. Also, Jason would be working at the library that day, and it made me anxious and confused not knowing what to expect from that or even what I wanted, whether I needed to sever things between us, the obvious choice, or if I should be clinging tighter, in case he was all I had left.

I watched as Loren and Alexander crossed the road to avoid walking directly next to a house being tented for termites. Once they had passed it, they crossed back. They were strolling half a block ahead of Finn and me. When we reached the tented house we did the same, crossed the road, over and back.

The multi-coloured tents had been popping up all over the neighbourhood in recent weeks. Even the Methodist church on the corner had been fumigated. Draped in a looming patchwork of blue and white canvas, the body of the brick-and-mortar building beneath had been concealed entirely except for the cross on the roof that stuck through, reminding everyone that a house of God still existed under there, and giving out strong tent revival vibes.

We'd experienced termite swarms in our living room the last two Mays. We told our landlord about it both times, but once the swarm had subsided we forgot about it till the next one. The second year, we were upstairs and missed the grand parade—saw only the remnants the next morning. I'd been sitting on the couch with Finn the first time. He was still very young, and I was watching TV and waiting for Dan to come home. It took me a while to realise what was happening, those tiny, winged creatures rising out of the floor around me as they made for the ceiling light, believing it to be the moon. I learned later that they were mating as they spun in the air, before shedding their wings, their plump torsos falling back to earth where they writhed and tried to burrow back into the floor. By the time I got Finn and myself out of the room, there were wings stuck to Finn's scabby cradle-cap head, a horrible toupee, and bits of termite in my mouth and ears.

When they reached the pond, Loren parked Alexander's stroller on the grass beside a pair of plastic lawn chairs someone had placed there for their own use. She helped Alexander from the stroller, then took his hand and led him to the edge of the water where the swans were circling. The artificial pond was in the centre of our neighbourhood. A thin, natural stream ran through it, north to south. The pond itself was a concrete construction, a bulge in the waterway wide enough for a small concrete and dirt island in the middle that had been planted with trees and shrubs. This was where the swans and geese lived. I'd heard there were also turtles and otters living nearby, though I'd never seen them. On the other side of the pond from where we were standing was a black plastic bin that contained special food for the birds. As Finn and I approached, I could hear Loren telling Alexander, No, they weren't going to feed the swans today, the swans weren't hungry.

'I know about the food,' she said, acknowledging I was there.

'Of course,' I said. I parked Finn's stroller beside Alexander's, engaged the brakes, but didn't let Finn out.

'I would never let him feed them his sandwich,' she added. She looked at me accusingly.

In his free hand Alexander was clutching a neat triangle of bread.

'Of course not,' I said.

'You're going to the library?' Loren said. Her voice had a disarming neutrality that somehow also swelled with judgment. She didn't appear to be able to turn this off. 'For Music & Movement.'

Alexander looked at his sandwich and then pointed at the swans and clearly enunciated, 'Swan, Mommy, swan is hungry.'

Finn was watching Alexander intently. He had inherited the dumb look on his face from my family—it was one I associated with Gerard's video game face. Finn was slightly older than Alexander, but I'd never heard him put that many words together, and with that kind of clarity. I hated to think that he was recognising this about himself now too. I looked, pained, from Finn, mouth open, spittle collecting at the tide of his bottom lip, to Alexander, who was gesturing so confidently. It was in the mid-eighties out and still early enough in the spring for this shift to feel steamy, my body not one hundred percent conditioned to the increasing warmth after the winter.

I registered then how overdressed Finn was in his overalls, T-shirt and sweatshirt.

'Is everything okay?' Loren asked.

I'd zoned out, staring at the surface of the pond, my eyes tracked on a discarded Payday wrapper. The white plastic skin was lying splayed and twisted up in a drift of leaves, mud and Spanish moss that had collected on the side of the pond.

I was also distracted by the depth of rosiness in Finn's cheeks. 'Yes,' I said. 'We're going to the library too.'

'You taught him,' Loren said. 'You were one of his teachers.'

This was really why I'd followed her—to ask about Calvin. I wanted to know everything. In the polite cold of the last few days and in the quiet dark hours of the night when I couldn't sleep, as I prowled the house, eating scraps of dried fruit and cleaning in unimportant ways—wiping crumbs off the corners of the couch, straightening magazines on the coffee table, arranging the cutlery in the drawer so it was all facing the same way—I'd thought about Calvin and his life, the one he'd lived and the one he might have lived, and I became increasingly concerned about the point where these paths diverged.

'What was it you taught him?' Loren said.

'I taught him writing,' I said.

'Xander,' Loren said, her detective's voice wobbling, revealing a rare warmth. 'Would you like another?'

'Yes,' Alexander said. '*Pease.*'

Finn still had his eyes trained on Alexander. He was completely mesmerised by this proper little man, with such good manners, and also dressed so appropriately for the weather.

'Was it really an accident?' I said.

I'd been thinking about what I'd heard at Perry's. If it was true that Calvin's death was accidental, I wanted to know how that was possible—the logistics of the events of that night, but also how it was *possible* in the bigger sense and what were you supposed to do with that? As a person, as a parent? I bent down to unbuckle Finn from his stroller and unclip him from his overalls so I could remove his sweatshirt. He didn't want to get out of the stroller, so I didn't push it, and buckled him back in.

'He was a nice kid,' I said.

Armed with a new triangle of sandwich, Alexander had lost interest in the swans. He was squatting on the grass picking with his free hand at a string of Spanish moss that had caught around the arm of one of the plastic chairs. His mother had been watching him, but now she looked up at me as if to say, *That's irrelevant, his being a nice kid,* which of course it was.

'I'm going to tell you what I know,' she said.

The swans had lost interest in us too. They'd swum off toward the far side of the pond, back through the murky water, slick with leaves and muck and a couple of discarded Zapp's bags. I'd recently received an email from the company that had a monopoly on all utilities for our city with the quarterly water quality report. The announcement said: 'Our drinking water continues to meet all federal and state requirements!'

'He left the party with two friends,' Loren said. 'They had an argument about bat flinging if you can believe it?'

'Bat flinging?' Then I realised I was picturing the wrong kind of bat. 'I don't know anything about baseball.'

'I played college ball,' Loren said. 'My wife did too. That's how we met actually—in a social league.'

'My husband and I met at a party above a car repair shop,' I said.

Loren smiled. For a moment the need to share these details from our lives appeared urgent, the tough stuff at the start of

134

the conversation falling away. I felt the yawn of it then, how lonely I was, a big ol' space still drumming away in me. Though as quickly as the conversation had opened, it shut back down.

'Calvin got out of the car,' Loren said. 'He didn't want to concede his opinion. He'd been drinking, but he could be stubborn, too, single-minded. Everyone I spoke to said he was a hard-working boy, polite, loved his family, but that he could also be quite the shithead.'

It was a weird thing to say. *Quite the shithead.* I didn't judge her though. I'd called Finn a shithead many times. I could also sense how much relaying this information upset her. Just as Calvin's death had made me fearful about Finn's life, I wondered how many of these kinds of cases had made her think about Alexander in new, worrying ways. She was a detective, but she was also a mother.

'He meant to walk the rest of the way home,' she said. 'Based on where he exited the vehicle, and no I don't have the foggiest notion what they were doing all the way down there. Stupid kids, stupid kids. Calvin was very drunk, I already said that. He was drunk enough, it seems, to stumble off the road. There're no streetlights down there. He didn't have his phone on him, he'd taken it out of his pocket at the party to go swimming, so he had no way to call anyone, no light. The only thing that makes sense in my mind is that somewhere along there he tripped and fell.'

'Gopher holes,' I said.

Loren looked at me blankly.

'And what,' I said, 'he knocked himself out?'

'More likely he got turned around,' she said. 'Enough to lose all sense of direction, which is how he ended up so deep in the forest. Where you found him.'

135

It was the first time she had acknowledged I'd been there that day and that we had seen each other. I'd been in the wrong place at the wrong time, and now this horrible thing was a part of my life. Perhaps this was what made Loren think I had earned a right to peek behind the curtain and to know what she knew.

'It'll be impossible to ever get a clear picture of what happened,' she said. 'Maybe we'll get some answers. Maybe not.'

This grey area, I could tell it didn't sit comfortably with her.

'My suspicion,' she said, 'is that he died of hypothermia. If he hadn't been so intoxicated, all that alcohol in his system, he might have survived the night.'

'What about—'

'His shoes? He'd left his shoes at the party—'

'Swimming,' I said.

'Swimming,' Loren said. 'One of the friends panicked and disposed of them later. He didn't want to get in trouble. He was scared what with the drunk driving and the rest that he would lose his scholarship. They can be good liars when they need to be, when the stakes are high enough.'

I took *they* to mean *everyone*.

'Was it so cold that night?' I said.

I couldn't believe this was how Calvin might have died. Hadn't he been able to hear the main road? See the headlights of passing cars? Find his way back and flag down one of those cars? And why didn't his friends come back and look for him? It was a detail that would plague me—that his friends had driven off and left him shoeless and phoneless on the side of the road, the State Park stretching in every direction, all because of an argument about baseball.

'It dropped to a sustained thirty-four,' Loren said.

It was also too silly—to die of the cold in Florida. I knew well enough how cold it could get here, for while our winters were brief it wasn't unusual for it to drop below freezing at night. We often had to drip our taps on January nights to stop the house's old pipes freezing and cracking. I knew these things, but it still felt like a prank. Calvin had lain in the dark, shivering, calling out, probably first for his friends, then for his parents, and no one had come. He had died exposed and scared, buttressed only by the weird sounds of the Florida night. It filled me with the worst feeling imagining this, a ball of dread so huge that I could feel it pushing against my gut, my lungs. I struggled to catch my breath.

'So, pretty cold,' Loren said. 'Survivable though.'

'Survivable,' I said with a murmur.

'Damp clothes, cold temp, alcohol in the system.'

Loren quietly listed these things as if she were a pathologist performing an autopsy. She was adding them to the already long list in her head of all the things that could harm her boy. I had a similar list in my head. I didn't want to be a fearful mother, one who kept her kid on a leash so short it cut in and hurt in other ways, but how did you protect against this unfortunate collection of events that on their own were nothing—swimming drunk, walking home alone drunk, being very, very drunk? What twenty-year-old hadn't done all these things and worse?

While this conversation took place, Alexander started rubbing the Spanish moss looped around the arm of the chair on his face. I remembered something I'd once heard about Spanish moss. Loren seemed lost in thought. She was looking in the direction of the geese on the island, her mind out there in the middle of the pond.

'Hey sweetie,' I said, crouching down where I stood, so I was more on Alexander's level. 'I think that's a bit yucky.'

'No, it's okay,' Loren said, snapping back into the scene.

'Doesn't, can't Spanish moss contain chigger larvae?'

'It's probably what you read,' she said, flatly, 'but it's not so.'

'Bird,' Finn said. This was the first word he'd attempted since we'd been standing beside the pond. He was watching the swans, who had begun to swim back in our direction.

'That's right,' I said. 'Water birds. Those are swans, and those are geese.'

'Last month a first responder colleague was called out to a residence where a number of children lived.' Loren's detective voice had returned. 'The woman was one of these S-A-H-M types'—she pronounced each of these letters individually, so it took me a while to get what she was saying—'and she wanted to use the Spanish moss for a craft project. Crafts?' She appeared both confused and disgusted. 'When my colleague arrived he found a young child severely burned. This woman had been boiling the moss, trying to clean it of the larvae that she had read about on a blog before she used it for these crafts, and the child had pulled the boiling pot off the stove and onto himself.'

'Oh no,' I said.

'Bird,' Finn said.

'Yes,' Loren said.

Alexander was busying himself half watching Finn and half trying to climb back into his stroller. He'd had enough.

'Thanks for telling me all this,' I said. 'About Calvin.'

'I shouldn't have,' Loren said.

'I appreciate that,' I said. 'I won't share it.'

'I'm sorry you had to see what you saw,' she said. 'I hope you can get over it one day.'

It was a blunt way to say this, but I valued the gesture of it all the same.

We walked to the library side by side in silence—four animals being pulled in the direction of the library on the Wednesday afternoon migration to Music & Movement. We weren't so different, Loren and me. What I'd previously not liked about her—how serious, cold, and judgemental she seemed—I knew I could also be those things. There was an intense worrying air around her, too, which didn't bring me any comfort, but rather made me feel my own worries and unhappiness a little deeper. As we reached the library doors, and I saw our reflections drawing in, two moms barely holding their bodies upright, I asked Loren if she and Alexander and Alexander's other mom would like to come to Finn's birthday party that Saturday.

'We're meeting at the Bat Conservancy's Spring Fair,' I explained, 'for something different, at ten o'clock.' She instantly declined. She was working, she said.

'That's a shame,' I said.

We rode the elevator in silence, parked our strollers outside the event room and took our seats around the floral comforter. We sat as far away from each other as possible. It was as if what had happened beside the pond—a brief but shared examination of a tragedy that wasn't ours but which we had both made our own, what had felt to me like the beginning of a friendship, one built on bad luck and fear, yes, but a friendship nonetheless—had in fact not happened at all.

I got hypothermia on the last day of swimming camp when I was fifteen. I thought I needed to swim faster, so I kept swimming long after my feet went numb, and I was struggling to breathe with each turn of my head. One stop at the end of the pool between sets, my coach saw how I was shivering. I was hoisted out of the water. I took a couple of steps before I collapsed on the pool deck. I remember being helped into the shower. I was told I argued while they put me under. 'See, I'm fine,' I said, from where I was sitting hunched and shaking against the cubicle wall. I don't recall how I got undressed and dressed again, or how I got to one of the rooms where we slept. I came to later in the morning lying on a mattress, tucked in with multiple wool blankets, the crinkle of silver mylar close to my skin. I got no sympathy though—all anyone wanted to talk about was the kid who had got himself stuck in the side of the pool. This was the memory that had first risen to the surface during Perry's dinner. I'd thought about it repeatedly in the days since. The kid from swimming camp, a skinny boy, bug-eyed and sweet, had been goofing around after training when one of the other kids dared him to climb into the open pocket in the side of the pool meant for overflow. It was a tight squeeze, but he made it. Then he couldn't get out. As he started to panic, he took on water. I never saw any of it, but I pictured that kid with only just enough room to breathe, hemmed in on three sides, the pool deck and grate pushing against his skull, water sloshing against his mouth and nose. Even imagining it made me feel claustrophobic.

If, like the ten days prior, the kid had gone to sleep that night on his mattress next to his mates, he might not have woken ever again. Instead, with camp finished, when he got home his parents initially reasoned he was exhausted, and so he ate his dinner and went to bed early. It was something in his mother's heart that told her there was more going on.

That, and earlier that month she had read an article about dry drowning—what were the odds? Unable to settle, she checked on her son throughout the night till she found him in the early hours barely breathing. He was resuscitated twice in the ambulance. Once he recovered, on the outside he looked like the same skinny kid, but he wasn't the same, not really. He took longer to get things done, and those enormous wide-set eyes that gave him such a lovely openness were often caught focused on something not in the room.

'You guys,' Chantelle said now.

She and Wren sat down next to Finn and me. She was nearly ten years my junior, with mind-blowing red hair that reached her hips. That day she was wearing a Meat Puppets T-shirt that she'd cut the sleeves off of, exposing on her upper arm a tattoo of Garfield tucked up in his bed box. The T-shirt had also been given a bleach tie-dye treatment, so the original black of the cotton, washed out ginger-to-white, looked burned, as if Chantelle had just been hauled from a housefire.

'We've missed you,' she said.

Though it was only a week since we'd seen each other at Music & Movement, it also seemed like an age had passed since the last time I was sitting in this windowless room playing mom.

'Same here,' I said. 'We made it.'

'How's your week been?' she asked. 'I hope it's a good teacher today.'

I hadn't called or messaged her all week. I'd thought I would tell her everything once I saw her, but now that we were here, I realised I wouldn't. Not yet anyway. Facing my good friend I couldn't stand the truth of it—my bad luck, my temper, my selfishness, the horrible events of the past week too much a reflection of my failings. I was afraid of her seeing that.

'It's been fine,' I said, my voice strained. 'You?'

I caught Loren's eye from across the comforter. She wasn't smiling. She was speaking to another mother, at the same time as she was gently, absently combing her fingers through Alexander's hair. She momentarily looked in my direction, but she didn't look at me. It seemed as if she was looking all the way through me.

'We went hiking,' Chantelle said. 'Wren and me. We saw a coyote.'

'There are coyotes in Florida?' I said distractedly, my attention snagged by what I thought was Jason's voice outside the door.

'We have coyotes in every state except Hawaii.'

Jason entered the event room. A memory of the last time we had been alone in his house came at me with a charge. I wanted to look away as he walked toward us. I wanted to not see how his T-shirt was tucked into his jeans, or his arms, the flex and veins and hair of them, how I knew they would feel to my touch.

'Y'all are lucky I volunteered to do a session over Spring Break,' he said to the room.

He smiled democratically, taking in each face except mine. He finished circling the comforter and, still without acknowledging me, sat cross-legged in the space directly to my left, so our knees were almost touching. I thought I would burst into flames, so that the last Finn would see of his mother would be what remained on the balding grey carpet—a few hard nuggets of bone, a drift of ash.

'You doing anything for the rest of Spring Break?' Chantelle said.

I spoke robotically. 'I heard about this beach, what's it called, Daytona?'

Jason began singing and signing the welcome song that kicked off every Music & Movement session, starting with the kid to his left.

'I love Daytona,' Chantelle said. *'It's time to say hello.* We're going kayaking. Tomorrow, just me and Wren.'

'Oh?' I said.

I was no longer fully in the room. I was thinking about the plastic container with the boiled eggs that last week I'd pitched into the sink. I recalled the sound it had made as it connected with the stainless steel, like the pop of a joint dislocating. That sound was a smooth flat stone pressed forever into the back of my skull, and it felt as if someone had just lifted that stone and then dropped it back in place. I winced at the reminder of it. I thought again about what had occurred to me in the second before I'd thrown the container, which was that what I'd done with Jason was in some way connected to Calvin.

The warmth of Jason's knee, I could almost perceive it across the inch that separated us. Across that space I thought I could also sense something of his person that I hadn't been able to sense before, of his tiredness, his unhappiness, his hopefulness. I both wanted to have this and didn't want it at all.

It was Alexander's turn to be welcomed. Loren had moved her hands so they were circling Alexander's bare soft arms. She was holding him gently, affectionately, and she was holding him fast, her fingers rigid like talons.

We welcomed Wren, and when it was Finn's turn, Jason leaned forward so he could make eye-contact with him. We'd been coming here for so long that it hadn't ever affected me in any particular way, Jason looking at Finn like that. Today

143

though, it didn't feel right. I was on the cusp of silently standing, heaving Finn over my shoulder, and walking fast from the room. Though I also thought that if I tried to stand, I wouldn't be able to. That even though I could see my legs, my wrists pressed to my knees, they weren't there or connected to me.

Chantelle waited till the middle of 'Five Green and Speckled Frogs' to tell me that during the week between Music & Movement sessions she and her boyfriend had broken up. She didn't possess an inside voice, so even *whispering* during a group singalong she was loud enough that a few other parents looked our way. When she'd relayed the most urgent details, she pulled back to see my reaction, which was one of concern because she was my friend and I didn't want to see her hurt, but also of poorly masked relief because I hated for her that her and Wren's lives would be forever tied to that man.

'Why didn't you tell me?' I said.

'Girl, I'm fine,' she said. 'He gave me Chlamydia.'

We were up to the verse where only two green and speckled frogs remained on the log. The few parents who had been looking our way now averted their eyes. I could feel Jason tense beside me.

'Made it pretty easy to leave,' Chantelle added. She sounded upbeat, as was her way. 'Anyway, I'm already taking more time to love myself.'

'You deserve better,' I said, and I meant it wholeheartedly. I meant it about her boyfriend, and I meant it about me and our friendship. I leaned forward and rubbed Wren's back. 'So does this guy.'

As we finished singing the fate of the last speckled frog, Finn stood and walked across the room to where a box of felt pens sat open on a low wooden table. He began pulling out the pens in fistfuls. While I was watching him, Jason stood to retrieve a book. I tried to catch his eye as he returned, but he continued to avoid looking in my direction. When he sat back down, the space between us had grown. As a physical measurement it was maybe an additional inch, but it felt like more. I turned back to Finn in time to see him remove the lid of a slime-green pen, and trip forward in such a way that his arm jerked, and he stabbed himself in the cheek. I stirred, placed my hands flat to the floor to get up. Finn didn't flinch. He didn't look at me, but casually wiped his fist against his cheek where there was now a long green mark. My pulse was racing out of pace with everything that was going on.

Calvin's death—it was absurd. It was a bunch of terrible carriages clipped one after the other on a slow-moving train that had painfully, unfairly tacked from hangover city to destination decomposing corpse in the forest. You couldn't dream it up, that shift. You definitely couldn't prepare for it. I thought of Calvin's mother, a woman I vaguely knew the shape of from a photo I'd seen in the news. I tried to imagine her receiving the information about the discovery of her son's body. Loren would be a poor choice for this task—she wouldn't be the person I would want telling me—but it's who I pictured. Calvin's mother wouldn't believe what she was hearing. She would laugh nervously. She would say there was a mistake. She would think she was having a bad dream. She would think she was inside her own nightmare *Truman Show*. She would get up and walk out of the room. She would walk out of the room and then she would turn around and walk back in again. She would see she had nowhere to go and that even if she left the house, the town, the county, the state, the country, eventually she would have to turn around and walk back into that room and sit down and take it, this joke of a horror show, which was in fact her real life.

'Has he moved out?' I asked Chantelle.

'Not yet,' she said. 'We're living at opposite ends of the trailer.'

'That seems untenable?' I said. 'Sharing that space.'

'I'm working on it,' she said. 'He can't use the front door. If he wants to come and go, he has to use the window in the spare bedroom. I made him put a stepladder out there. He's also not allowed to use the bathroom. One day soon, he'll stop coming back.'

She said this with a sense of finality. This was her plan and it would work. She could wait. I'd never known anyone like Chantelle.

'You didn't tell me about the prescribed burn,' she said.

'No,' I said.

'My high school boyfriend's parents' house burned down after being struck by lightning. They were asleep when the fire started. No, the house didn't get struck, it was a tree next to the house, which caused the fire.'

'How awful,' I said.

'He was the person who got me hooked,' she said. 'He's dead now, but that fire, he and his whole family walked away from it without a scald between them.'

Conversations with Chantelle often took these turns. She shared these details from her life with a tone that was no graver than what she used to talk about buying laundry detergent or how Michael Stipe had the ideal dimensions for a man. More than once she had explained away the curvy nature of her past with the immense pressure and expectations of her parents and how she'd been unable to handle it. They'd wanted her to become an orthopaedic surgeon and she'd had the grades but not the desire to pursue such a high-stakes life.

We were onto an uncanny version of 'Wheels on the Bus' when my phone started to vibrate. It was Dan. Chantelle nodded toward Finn, suggesting she had it under control. I was reluctant to leave Finn, even for a minute. A montage had started playing in my head of all the ways he could injure himself with those pens, so that by the time I was standing outside the door to the event room I was picturing a bruised porcupine boy, pens protruding from every orifice. Dan wanted to know if I could swing by the bodega on the way home for a sandwich. I knew this to mean he would first like me to check the warmer for sausage burritos, otherwise, he would settle for a chicken salad baguette.

'You could've texted that,' I said.

'Get chips too,' he said.

'Do you want this for dinner or what?' I said. I had no patience for him or this request right now.

'Just to eat,' he said.

'You gave me a fright,' I said. Only once I'd said it did I see this was where some of my irritability stemmed from. It was the irritability of concern. 'You okay?'

'Yep,' he said. 'You?'

'Yep.'

Neither of us sounded convincing. The cool silences of the past few days had been periodically broken with these questions. I did want to know how Dan was—as I waited for him to broach what needed to be broached, I worried about whether he was managing, how he was hurting. When we were standing next to each other in the kitchen, or lying quietly in bed pretending to read, I wondered about him as if he were far away and unreachable. Then I would see that he was right there. 'Are you okay?' I would ask, trying to get a feel for the space between us. He would reply, 'Yep, you?' Back and forth. It seemed to me that both of us were aware of the other's presence in a new way. We were two house birds taking nervous turns scraping the dust and dirt from the other's feathers, which was a form of communication, a sign of bonding, but was that how far we'd fallen?

'How's music club going?' Dan said now. This was the real reason for his call.

'Finn's not even remotely interested,' I said. On hearing myself say my boy's name out loud, something ripped through me. I shifted so I could see back inside the event room. Finn was where I'd left him with the pens, happy and unbothered.

'No kidding,' Dan said, with a swell of pride. Finn's lack of interest in singing that disconcerting version of 'Wheels on the Bus' with the *cool youth pastor* was a kind of proof of Dan's position in our family.

It had seemed impossible that Dan would leave. The security I felt with him had made it easier to do what I'd done. I'd thought there would be no consequences. Dan was a deeply non-confrontational person, but that 'No kidding', while throwaway, also contained a well of anger and hurt. It was something I'd done throughout our relationship, I saw it then: I'd mistaken Dan's quiet acceptance for a lack of feeling or care.

Once very late at night in a city I haven't lived in for many years, I walked home through a long, narrow tunnel built for buses to cut through the middle of a hill. The tunnel was four hundred yards long and there were no lights. I was very drunk.

A part of me wanted to do it just so I could say I'd done it. But I had also had an argument with the guy I was sleeping with and I was in a sulk. As I walked and then ran through the darkness, a partially consumed mince-and-cheese pie in my hand, the light at the other end feeling for the longest time like it wasn't getting any brighter or bigger, and the light behind me feeling equally far away, neither exit increasing in size, I thought I was going to die. At one point I stopped and began running back in the direction I'd come from, but again I had this feeling like I was running towards nothing. Though the earth was there and hard beneath my feet, I also couldn't really feel it. I was running towards nothing and in nothing. And so I turned again, and continued in my initial direction. I thought I was already dead. When I finally popped out the other end of the tunnel, sweating, and my skin prickled with the cold and fright, I stopped beneath a streetlamp and caught my breath. I laughed, nervously and loudly. It was the laughter of a person who was very drunk but also very ill at ease in herself and her life. I thought I'd had a near-death experience. It didn't fill me with anything close to calmness or serenity.

Back inside the library room, all the parents had taken up the edges of a large piece of fabric—a multi-coloured parachute without its strings. This was the last musical number of the session. The parachute was being pulsed up and down while the kids danced and ran beneath it to 'Strawberry Fields'. In the time I'd been finishing my conversation with Dan, Finn had left his pens and moved so he was under the parachute too. He wasn't dancing, but rather crouching and watching the colours wave in and out, sucking so close to his face that I suspected this was what he liked most, to feel the whisper of cloth near his skin.

I moved to take my place between Chantelle and Jason, but there wasn't space for me—all edges of the parachute were accounted for. I stood back and watched. Chantelle was laughing as Wren spun in circles. The other parents were smiling and laughing with their kids too. I could no longer see Finn—he was crouched directly in front of Jason, obscured by him. I looked at the back of Jason's head, the slip of his neck, the thick rounding of his back, his leather belt tight against his hips and his butt—it was a good butt, I hadn't thought so before, but I thought so now. It shook me up, looking at this man on whom I'd gambled the other parts of my life. It worried me to think of the anger in Dan's voice, though part of me was pleased too. I thought maybe I wanted to see more of it. Was that the proof I needed of my position in our family? Was the best I could hope for that I should mess up, and that my husband should care? In Dan's tone, I'd also sensed some freedom. This was a new thing.

Jason looked over his shoulder. He'd been smiling, but as our eyes met, his face fell. Something had shifted. It was only a matter of time. Saturday night at Perry's had sped it up. Jason had seen me in a wider context—of my marriage, of our extended community of acquaintances—that was part of it. I also thought he had seen something in me he didn't like—in the way I'd disappeared and returned, in the way I'd held myself in that room and interacted with Dan, Perry, and the others, in the way I'd said what I'd said about Calvin. We'd been pretending we weren't real people, with real lives, worries, edges.

What did I know about Jason? I knew he had spent the first twenty-three years of his life in Alabama. I knew that he'd written, illustrated and published a book for children. I knew that he liked the novels of Thomas Bernhard and flat-leafed houseplants, that though he wasn't vegetarian, he couldn't stand the look and smell of raw meat, that he was right-handed, that he exfoliated, toned, and moisturised, and that he had, like Dan and Perry, been a smoker but had quit cold turkey the day after his thirty-first birthday. I knew he'd studied sociology and philosophy in college. I knew both of his parents were dead and that he was circumcised. These things didn't make a whole person, though soon his life and the wider corners of it would come into view. While I had the beginnings of an idea of what that might look like, I didn't want the edges of my life to meet the edges of this man's life any more than they did now: 'Strawberry Fields', the lift and swish of a thin sheet of fabric. I hadn't wanted to fall in love. And though I could smell the souring of the light and fun of our relationship, the bad scent a warning of something in the early stages of decomposition— for we couldn't continue this way forever, one way or another it would become a different thing—still I wanted to push on.

I could never just quit something. At school, I'd carried on with many of my extra-curricular activities even after I'd begun to loathe them. It had been the same with men. I was never the one to leave. I clung on, hoping to squeeze the last breath out of what was left. Even the man who spent his days photographing blank concrete walls, I couldn't leave.

Almost immediately from the moment Jason first covered my hand with his own dry, warm hand, the good feeling of him, the excitement and the lust, was knotted through with a bad feeling too. Before, when I'd imagined something like this happening, *an affair*, I'd assumed this bad feeling would be guilt. I still didn't feel guilty. Instead, the bad feeling that accompanied me was the knowledge that Jason would eventually go away. The anxiety of it, wondering what he would take from me or of me, I hadn't experienced since before I'd met Dan, though with each of the men I could recall from the bedrooms of my twenties, our time together had also been bound in this way, in smaller and larger amounts. Dan was the only one with whom I'd never felt the rope of fear of an inevitable end. I'd been so relaxed and comfortable in the warm bath of our relationship that it had made me complacent and selfish with his love. With Jason, I was still trying to live an independent life while being simultaneously terrified that I would have to live that independent life alone. Except now I was thirty-six and I wasn't alone, so why did I need it, and why was I still so afraid?

'What're your plans for tonight?' I said to Chantelle.

Most of the kids and caregivers had dispersed. No one was interested in sticking around for free play this week. Jason was bundling up the parachute.

'Po' boys and *Stranger Things*,' Chantelle said. 'Then an early night. Kayaking tomorrow remember.'

'Right, cool,' I said. Something in my voice caught me. Was I annoyed at Chantelle?

Though it appeared that she had easily picked herself up from the disaster of her relationship with Wren's father, I knew that wasn't true. What seemed like a shrug on her part was really her way of coping and working through the hurt. Seeing her like this though, made me acknowledge what likely lay ahead with Jason, and I hated being made to think about it, the bad feeling.

'You?' Chantelle said. Her tone told me she'd also heard the frustration in my voice.

'I don't know,' I said, distinctly quieter, kinder. 'Maybe I'll see my lover.'

Chantelle made a face. It wasn't like me to make a joke like this. I couldn't look Jason in the eye either.

'Okay, we're outta here,' Chantelle said. She was running late to meet her mother.

'We're outta here too in a minute,' I said.

I watched her lead Wren by the hand. She stopped at the door and turned to face me, then smiled. 'Don't forget to use protection,' she said. Her voice was round and jokey, trying to smooth over more than one thing.

A heat blossomed in my cheeks. The other remaining mother in the room looked at Chantelle and then me and then back inside her diaper bag without changing her expression. I tried to shake the embarrassment off, turned to Finn. He was building towers with some coloured blocks.

'You're doing a great job sorting those,' I said.

I couldn't bring myself to sit down. I was cemented to the spot—suspended between whatever was happening behind me in Jason's corner of the room, and myself as a mom. Finn was about to place a red block on the all-yellow tower he'd made. He stopped, repositioned it on the top of the other reds. He was invested in this task. He was already getting used to playing solo, the repetition of this slowly hardening into a personality trait. Finally, the last mother and her kid left. When I turned around, I saw Jason standing in profile to me. He was shuffling a pile of books as if they were playing cards.

'Are you angry with me?' I said, finally.

Jason looked up. 'That's something a child would say.'

The question and response were humiliating. Jason didn't appear disgusted though. He looked more confused.

'What?' I said. It wasn't an accusation, it was a plea.

'I prayed I'd see you today,' he said.

Two months ago, if I'd taken any time to think about this, if it had even been something I would use to organise my world, I would have said there was only one person whose prayers I would ever care to know.

I'd feared the sex would be bad, that it was a mistake to think a stranger could know enough about what I liked for it to be worth it. The first time, I'd come so quickly. Jason had loosened something in me with ease. The sureness and pressure of his movements, the way he'd held me as my body began to fold against the weight of my own breath, the most surprising thing about it had been its familiarity. I'd also been concerned about what Jason would see and how I would feel to him. Before each visit to his house, I'd tentatively probed about with my fingers, feeling out the ridges and wings of scar tissue—what remained of the trail Finn had left behind as he emerged hard and fast in the end, a fist punched through a sheet of printer paper—and I'd tried to hold on to what it meant, the good of it, my boy, but I'd only been able to for a second. I'd almost asked Jason straight up, the words on the tip of my tongue: 'Do I feel weird? Different?' But different compared to what?

Dan had said I didn't feel any different. He didn't think I'd changed and, I realise now, this was its own kind of rejection, a different kind of betrayal. I'd become too many things to Dan, that was our problem, and we piled those things one on top of the other, so it all became *growth* and *life*. I was too many layers of person to him and he'd gotten used to it. Being a wife and a mother, those were the heavy ones. Along with all the bad moods, all the times I'd lost my temper, of which last Thursday night was only the most recent, the times I'd spoken to him low and ferociously with ugly words, and then the long pale days

154

in between those days and the good ones. Those layers, I wore them like a huge musty coat of animal pelts. Dan had a coat too. And there was no way to remove our coats and just be two people with bodies wanting each other. Though what Dan and I had was meant to be better, more meaningful, all those layers that were wrapped around us, they were also between us, in the way. The big stuff and the minutiae of eight years together, our love for each other, which wasn't even a very long time, we were still so close to the beginning really, was what made Dan my home. Everything that had felt good and secure about him, the things that I believed I still needed, didn't want to not have, all those nautical ropes tied up in lovely tight knots, I also needed to be free of. I wanted to slide my feet across the deck of that boat—my boat—reach down, undo those ropes, and let them fall away.

This man knew nothing of my layers. To him I was merely an outline of a woman. I'd been simplified and that had lightened me, for a moment.

'It was wrong,' Jason said now. 'A bad idea.'

'Wrong?' I said.

'I thought it didn't matter,' he said. 'I thought I was above it.'

'Above it?' I said. 'What, like God?'

He didn't flinch. The ease with which he deflected my words made me suddenly think that he'd been married, or as good as married, though it was unbelievable that I didn't know this for sure. What had we spoken about when we were together? We'd talked fast. Not about music or books, but about Alabama's forests, Florida's forests, where in the country we'd camped, New Mexico's mesas, the hugeness of the sunset in Big Bend, Shenandoah in the fall. We'd spent a disproportionate amount of time discussing our favourite kind of horse, though Jason had only ridden one twice, and I had only ridden one once. I couldn't go past a scruffy wild one like you could find down on the prairie. Jason liked a sleek brown one with a blond mane, the colour of horse that looked like a tanned and sun-bleached beach bum. When he'd said this, he'd done so with an absurd sincerity that had made me laugh, which had left him confused, which had made me reassure him, which had made him laugh too, which looking back now, was probably it, the moment.

'It was wrong,' he said now. 'A bad idea.'

'You already said that,' I said.

'Hmm,' he said.

I thought then of the long, dark tunnel I'd foolishly run through that cold night in my twenties. That *hmm*, Jason's *hmm*, took me to the middle of that tunnel. Once again, I was stopped and unsure whether to continue forwards or turn back. I wanted to erupt with a hideous burst of laughter, but I couldn't find it, the laughter of the uneasy, the relieved, the happy, of any of those things. I couldn't conjure it. It was only arms and legs and it wasn't meant to be worth a damn, which was an argument for not fucking around, though it could also be one for fucking around, why not? Even if what Jason had seen of me was so little, and even if there was much more of me he hadn't seen or would never see, I'd let him in. I didn't believe that he could give me the life I wanted, but for some reason that didn't matter. He'd felt around inside my body, and I saw now with some horror that I'd cleared a space for him in my heart. What was already in there had been pressed to the sides, like clothes shoved to the far ends of a closet, to make room to hang this man and his prayers.

It was my own fault for being too porous.

156

'Sweetie,' I said, crouching down so I was on Finn's level, 'time to say bye-bye to the blocks. Can you say bye-bye?'

It took Finn a long time to arrive at his words. The choppy sea of his speech, and the growing impatience I sensed in myself as I waited for him to pitch the words high enough for me to catch, it dragged me under. He finally stood and waved at his three neat towers. He extended his arms towards me. I picked him up. Once again, I felt that twinge in my lower back—a pinpoint of comfort, a thing to hold on to. When I reached the door, I turned. Jason was watching us go. I thought I'd never been this angry with someone before.

'Congratulations, Jason,' I said.

He didn't speak, he just looked at me.

I couldn't read a single thing on his face. Then I could.

Dan was waiting for us on the front steps when we got home. I couldn't recall one time in all the years I'd known him that he'd greeted me like this. I didn't ask why he was home early from the workshop, and he didn't offer this information. He smiled for Finn, but not for me. I handed Dan his burrito and his chips, and the three of us went inside. Dan sat on the couch and slowly, meticulously peeled back the foil of his burrito. Finn joined his father, a toy truck in each hand. They had a conversation about the trucks. Dan asking the questions, Finn answering in his own language.

The night before, I'd had another nightmare about Calvin. I'd woken to the warm darkness of our bedroom in a sweat, my body rigid. I'd ventured downstairs, where I turned on the kitchen faucet and filled a glass with water though there was already a full glass sitting on my bedside table. Every night since the burn, this was the thing that would get me out of bed.

I would wake from a bad dream thirsty for fresh water. I'd say it over and over in my head as I went: *fresh water, fresh water.* It had become the only means by which I could find my way back to sleep. I didn't like being awake in the middle of the night. It took me back to the many months of Finn's life when I was up breastfeeding, soothing, alone. I wasn't a night owl. I liked the day. Sunlight. When I'd drained that glass of water, I filled another, did some tidying—rinsed a dirty plate and knife on the kitchen counter, put some felt pens left on the table back in their container—then I returned to the kitchen. I stood over the stainless-steel sink and I thought: They're upstairs, Finn, Dan. You're downstairs and they're upstairs, but you can go back up the stairs any time you want. Finish your water, then go. But I couldn't. I remained there, standing at the sink, for the longest time.

This was the life I'd wanted. Everything I could see from where I was now leaning against the doorway, Finn and Dan, all of it, I'd sought it out. None of it had been an accident. Yet I could barely stand to face it.

The summer I was five years old, it had taken a month of visiting the school pool and Gerard's coaxing before I would push off from the wall in the deep end. I'd never been brave, and yet, I'd done things. The rocks at the south end of the beach where I grew up jutted into the sea far enough that on a big swell day, the waves would crash and froth over them. It was impressive from a distance. Up close, to avoid being prematurely swept from the slippery surface of the rocks, you had to stand sideways, plant your feet, and muster all your faith. When you were ready to jump, in order to avoid smashing your skull on the rocks concealed by the water, you had to get the timing right, catching the swell perfectly on its way up. No second guessing, fins, one in each hand, you and your heart, you had to go for it.

I did these things, jumping from the rocks in high crashing seas, because people expected me to, and because I kept doing them, they kept expecting me to do them. Not once in all the years of living in that house with my parents and Gerard and swimming at that beach did I ever tell someone that it scared me to death to do those things. I didn't want to be scared to death. I haven't watched a horror movie since the midnight premiere of *The Blair Witch Project* in 2000, a night that still comes to me in flashes—I'll never get over it.

On the days when the surf was even too rough for surf life saving practice, we would retreat with our swim gear, boards and skis to the wide, deep dam in the back of the forest, not far from the pond where I'd forgotten my watch. The calm water of the dam, a murky swimming pool full of eels, I didn't mind. When the other kids complained about how boring it was in the dam compared to the sea, I exhaled in relief. For starters, I could never not see the shore, and it had comforted me greatly to know I could swim the distance.

Jason had opened something in me. I didn't know what to do about it. This time with Dan, was it just a bad time? Was there another side? Did I simply expect too much from this man who was a good man and who had never not supported me, not really, not unless I was splitting hairs? A man who every morning, no matter how we were, made a point of asking me how I'd slept and then listened to my answer? And which was Dan and which was Jason, the sea, the dam, the dam, the sea? It seemed obvious, the answer to that question, but maybe not?

'Calvin's death,' I said, from where I was still standing at the edge of the living room, 'it looks like it was an accident after all.'

'Really?' Dan said. He didn't look up from his burrito. 'What did you hear?'

'One of the detectives, I saw her today. She filled me in.'

'Filled you in in what way?'

Dan lifted his head and our eyes met. I knew then that this conversation wasn't going to go the way I wanted it to. I thought again about the kid I'd known who had got stuck in the side of the pool and nearly drowned. Shitty things happen to people all the time. What about this, this disaster that I'd part made and part fallen into, the undoing of the last week? What would this time really do to Dan and me? Could it fix us, or would it be the thing that meant we were never again quite right?

'She told me everything she knew,' I said.

'That seems unethical?' Dan said.

I didn't reply.

'What do you want to do for dinner?' Dan said.

'There's pesto in the fridge,' I said, my voice free of any emotion.

'Pasta's good.' He sounded chipper.

All I had to do was boil the water. Throw in the pasta. Strain the pasta. Stir in the pesto. Serve it up. It was the world's easiest dinner. It was a dinner easy and stupid enough for a college kid to make. Calvin could have made it. All my other students too. Calvin's corpse could make it. The sack of bones and meat of him could roll and slip its way across the room and open the fridge and the cupboard and turn on the faucet and the stove, and yet I thought I would be crushed under the weight of that task.

'I have to go,' I said. Those words, it was as if they were being pulled from me on a long fleshy string. I sounded possessed. 'Where're the keys?'

'What keys?' Dan said.

'The car keys,' I said.

Dan handed them over without a question.

9.

The afternoon Finn broke his teeth, when we finished booking a follow-up appointment, I needed to make a bathroom stop, my bladder still working as well as a sodden cardboard box. Finn and Dan went ahead. When I reached the car, I found Dan sitting rigid behind the wheel, staring out the front windscreen. As I buckled my seatbelt, I perceived something like a quiver to him—not in his hands or bottom lip, nothing as concrete as that, it was more like he'd shaken himself out of focus. It made me think anything could happen next, that he could cry, yell, laugh, collapse in a heap. Though it was unnerving to observe Dan short-circuiting with worry in this uncharacteristic way, I'd also been pleased to see some proof of it.

Now as I descended our front steps, car keys in hand, I thought I noticed something like this again. He'd been playing chipper, but the way he'd sat and watched me walk toward him with my hand extended revealed something I hadn't previously been able to see. In the blink of time it took the car keys to fall from his hand into mine, I saw it and I felt I should stay. It was a strong feeling, and yet. Staying, going, going, staying. My body knew where we were going before I'd even formed a clear thought about it. Once I was behind the wheel of the car, I logged on to the university's online teaching platform from my phone and scanned the student assignments from previous semesters till I found the resume assignment Calvin had submitted in the fall. As I hoped, there in the top right-hand corner was his permanent address, the house where his parents lived, in a quiet throughway town north of Orlando. It was approximately two hours away. The sun would still be up when I got there. This was what I was rushing towards now. I needed to tie something off, and this was it. I was going to pay my respects.

For a large portion of the drive I crossed a national forest. I found myself pretending that all those acres of Florida pines were New Zealand pines, till my view was interrupted by highway signs exhibiting the silhouettes of bears and panthers. I passed orange groves, gun shops and shooting ranges, and spotted a hundred turkey vultures circling above a farm advertising gator jerky. I also glimpsed the remnants of a prescribed burn. A tiny bell rang in my head at the sight of the smouldering, smoky earth. That view and what it meant, of course it took me back to Calvin. It also oddly warmed me.

Calvin's parents lived on a quiet street that, though only a breath from a major city and highway, had the special Florida quality of being not quite urban, suburban, or rural, but existing in a liminal space of all and none of these definitions. There was a thin strip of white sidewalk on one side of the street. On the other side the road ended where the front lawn of each property began. There were low wire fences, shrubs and trees dividing

163

properties, many of which had white concrete driveways and lawns pocked with ant mounds. A state park was close by and, as with so many places in Florida, the intersection of human life and the natural world became a dense weaving together of both, so there was both the feel of the uncluttered suburb as well as so many trees, so much green, leaching in. When Dan and I returned home the spring of our road trip to Texas, we found our apartment full of frogs, both alive and dead. As we shooed them out, swept them up, we counted twelve in total. During our four-week absence, the frogs had made our house their home and their graveyard. In Florida nature always found a way in.

Many of the houses in this neighbourhood were squat, made of cinderblock. As I drove slowly up Calvin's street, I could see glimpses of backyard swimming pools behind some of the larger Sixties weatherboards. These houses were nothing to look at, many in need of a repaint, several bearing American flags, some with Trump–Pence flags, but people lived here, maybe even loved living here. I didn't stop the first time I reached my destination. As I turned a corner, I passed a trio of young kids on scooters, and another trio of older kids standing next to a red F-150, the two boys smoking, the girl, legs long and brown in the tiniest cut-offs, scoffing Nerds. I experienced a wave of nostalgia so strong at that sight, not for my own teens or the long summers spent similarly hanging around. No, it was a nostalgia for this life, this town, which wasn't the town where we lived but that still evoked what I'd started to picture as Finn's Florida life, his childhood and his teens, the handful of golden years we would get to have him in our home.

I'd spent the whole drive planning what I would say to Calvin's parents. I saw myself walking up the front steps and knocking on the door. Would I be invited inside? Did I want to go inside? Driving past their house a second time, I saw how crazy this was. A few doors down, I pulled over and put the car in park. These people, they had not only lost their son, he had been left out in the forest to rot. I thought again of what I'd seen, not even a week ago, the shape of what was left of Calvin's body slowly forming in my line of vision. I'd done my best to bat it away, and to hold on to Calvin as I'd remembered him from my classroom, a whole boy with his body, dreams, and future still intact. It was still there though, the vivid picture of him in the forest. It had a smell and it had a sound.

I wanted to call Dan. As I tried to unlock my phone, I saw my hands were shaking. I slid the phone into my pocket. I switched off the car's ignition, undid my seatbelt, and got out. Though I had a bad feeling about it, the need to go was too huge. This was something I had to do.

Calvin's parents' house was a large weatherboard, painted white with a grey roof. Two SUVs were parked in the driveway, each with University supporter stickers affixed to their bumpers and side windows. The cars were shiny, ringed by the last of a not-yet-evaporated soapy puddle. As the driveway turned into a path leading to the front door, the lawn opened into a rock garden planted with succulents. Along the narrow strip of porch were more succulents in white ceramic pots. The screen door was open, hooked back to the wall. A green plastic wreath decorated with holly, grinning snowmen and a golden *Merry Christmas* hung from the front door. It looked dusty and brittle, too long out in the sun now.

A moment after I knocked, a girl I assumed was Calvin's sister opened the door. Unlike Calvin, she wore glasses—over-sized black frames that did nothing to hide the family brow. It was impossible to tell whether she was a popular girl or a nerd or somewhere in between. She was a teenager, maybe fifteen, her acne not so bad, her hair long and dark and clean.

'Hi?' she said. She wore braces on her top and bottom teeth.

She looked from my face to my empty hands. She didn't appear surprised or even curious. I wasn't the first person to arrive on the front doorstep like this, maybe not even the first person today.

'You don't know me,' I said.

'No,' she said. She shifted her weight onto one hip. She was wearing short pink chinos and a white tank top under a half-zipped grey hoodie. She looked over her shoulder into the house. Her hair was pulled back in a blood-red velour scrunchie. 'Mom,' she called out. 'It's a lady.'

She didn't wait for her mother to arrive. As she disappeared down the hallway, I saw what I'd not been able to see when she was standing so close to me. Her legs, from her ankles to where they disappeared into her shorts, were scarred by what must have been deep and very painful burns. Calvin's dream, the life he'd wanted as a biomedical engineer—*new and better synthetic skins*—his younger sister, here, had been his motivation.

I only waited at the door alone for a few seconds, but it was enough time to think I should leave. As with the afternoon of the prescribed burn and many other times recently, however, I felt stuck, unable to move.

'Can I help you?' Calvin's mother said. I recognised her from the photo I'd seen in the news. She, too, looked down at my hands, which held nothing, no gift, no offering.

'You don't know me,' I said again. It was the one truth I had to share.

Calvin's mother blinked, waited. She was petite. A fit-looking woman with the physique of a long-distance runner. She was wearing light makeup, though she was dressed casually in shorts and tank top like her daughter. She, too, wore glasses— oblong wire frames that looked twenty years old. Her hair was styled in a neat wavy bob.

'I was one of Calvin's university teachers,' I said. 'I wanted to pay my respects'—that phrase, it sounded hollow and meaningless now—'to let you know how sorry I am.'

'How did you get our address?' she said.

I don't know why I hadn't anticipated this question. I couldn't immediately remember how I'd got it. 'One of Calvin's assignments?' I sounded flustered. 'Your address was on it.'

She nodded, didn't smile. 'What did you teach him?'

'Writing,' I said.

'That's good,' she said.

'He was a really smart, lovely kid,' I said.

She nodded again. She already knew that he was smart and lovely, a boy with good manners who knew what it meant to work hard and to want to contribute something meaningful to the world, a boy who could also be a shithead. She didn't need me, a complete stranger, to tell her these things. The silence was huge. What had I expected? For this woman to be grateful that I'd driven this far, these whole two-and-a-bit hours, to stand on her front doorstep and tell her something she already knew? Calvin's father appeared behind her. I hadn't seen him coming. I knew he was Calvin's father because he was the bringer of the family brow. Here was the man Calvin would have grown into, standing behind his wife. He appeared more tired than quizzical.

'We're about to leave somewhere,' he said.

It was an excuse he'd used a hundred times in the last

month to get unwelcome guests like me to leave. Calvin's sister re-emerged from the hall and her father put his arm around her, pulled her close. The three of them appeared as a tight unit.

'I was in the forest,' I said. I addressed Calvin's mother as I spoke. 'I was there when they found him.'

'We're still waiting on the DNA results,' Calvin's father said. He didn't sound convincing, but he wasn't yet ready to face the fact that what was left of his boy was lying in the university morgue.

'Of course,' I said.

'You were with the burners?' Calvin's mother said. She wanted to know more.

'I was,' I said.

'What did you see?' Her voice was hard, fraught.

I'd seen what she had been unable to see, and likely discouraged from seeing—her son, where he had died, what remained of him. I saw how much she wanted me to answer her. She wanted to know the details—even if it killed her, she wanted to know. It became clear to me then that I hadn't come all this way just to pay my respects. Though I still couldn't say exactly what I was there for, if this was it, or if it was something else.

The night Finn was born, one of the maternity nurses in the room had asked me if I wanted a mirror to help me push. This scene came to me so whole and bright, it was as if I was momentarily experiencing it again. I firmly declined the mirror. I didn't want to see how my obstetrician used the short breaks between pushes to desperately stretch me out, the same action you might use to stretch raw pastry around the rim of a pie dish. I didn't want to see Finn's large head crown, already with a full scalp of Dan's family's black hair, the half of Finn that wasn't me presenting itself immediately.

I hadn't wanted to see any of it. I'd believed it would ruin me. I'd thought about this periodically in the two years since that night, and now here I was thinking about it again. I wished I could go back and answer differently. I hadn't seen any of those things, but Dan had and I wondered if I'd given him a glimpse of something I shouldn't have. The meat of me, but also other parts of me, my secret life, all the things I'd done and all the things I still wanted to do, my hard pebble-sized desires. It was absurd, but when Finn emerged, I felt they also come bursting out of me with the last drips of amniotic fluid and blood, for Dan to desperately try and avoid looking at. How could he not, though? How could he look away when it was all just there? To reveal the parts you didn't want to reveal, the parts that also maybe shouldn't be revealed, that was marriage, I got that. Maybe it was humbling. Maybe instead of worrying about it I was supposed to feel that—humbled.

'What did you see?' I'd asked Dan repeatedly in the days and months after that night. He couldn't really tell me.

'I saw him,' I said to Calvin's mother now.

'Tell me,' she said, as she took my arm.

And then the four of us were sitting around the kitchen table. I looked from Calvin's mother, desperate and pleading, to Calvin's sister, who looked as if she had been hypnotised, her eyes blank and trained on something a thousand light-years away. Waves of panic flickered across his father's brow, like a man who was realising over and over too late that the car he was driving was going too fast for an approaching sharp corner, so all that was left to do was grip the steering wheel and hope for the best.

'No, I'm not an experienced burner,' I said. 'It was my first time.'

Calvin's mother nodded as if there was some value in this detail.

'I don't know that I have anything new to contribute,' I said.

I was already looking for a way out. How I got from standing on the front porch to sitting around the kitchen table was hazy. I can't recollect any details of that short journey. I also can't recall a single thing about the interior of that house, what was hanging on the walls, what the furniture was like, what scents and sounds hung in the air.

'Was he very far into the woods?' Calvin's mother said.

Calvin's father made a face suggesting this was something they had already discussed at length. Calvin's sister focused on picking off the tiny, pilled balls from the sleeve of her hoodie. She had already harvested enough to create a soft grey pyre on the tabletop. The height and breadth of the mound was unnervingly large and disproportionate to how long I thought we'd been sitting there.

'He was,' I said. 'Quite a way in.'

'He always had a bad sense of direction.' She spoke thoughtfully and warmly. Remembering this detail about her son must have transported her to a time when he was still alive. She wanted to remain there for a moment.

'We haven't been allowed to see him,' she said, finally. She was back from where she'd been, sitting again in the cold, hard present of it.

Calvin's father reached across the table and placed his hand on his wife's shoulder. He gripped it hard.

'I think we're done here,' he said.

'What did you see?' Calvin's mother said once more.

That's all she wanted to know. She needed a picture of how her son had been found, not because it could give her clues as

170

to how he'd died, that was pointless and useless now, but rather in the hope that it would show her something about how he'd lived. She wanted to know if she'd done okay by him.

All I could think of was the phrase that had echoed in my mind the afternoon of the burn—*a grisly scene*—and I knew then why I'd come. I'd wanted to tell this woman, this person I didn't know, precisely what I'd seen. I'd thought that if I could describe the state of her son's body for her in enough detail, maybe he would up and leave from my mind, and return fully to his nest in hers, and that space in mine would be free again. I'd pinpointed finding Calvin's body as the beginning of too much undoing, of my quiet unhappiness growing into a deafening unhappiness. I'd thought that if I could get rid of him, I would be able to return to some earlier state where the parts of my life were knowable and manageable. Life wasn't a narrow bus tunnel through a hill though. There wasn't an option to turn back to the time before, to what I still thought of as the easier calm of Dan and me. I knew that then, and I knew that telling Calvin's mother what I'd seen wouldn't exorcise that boy or change a thing. There was only the other side. So, what was on the other side?

'There was a lot of smoke,' I said. 'I honestly couldn't see much.'

'He still slept on his front,' she said. 'The same way he did when he was a toddler. His arms like this.'

I watched as she pressed her arms to her chest and balled her hands into fists up under her chin. She shut her eyes tight. This was how she'd chosen to think of her son as he took his last breaths. She'd allowed herself to imagine that he'd gone to sleep in the forest, his belly to the earth, his eyes closed in a dream. I wanted to tell her this was what I'd seen, that I'd found Calvin in the pose of a child sleeping, to hand her that reassurance. I couldn't find the words though. Because I didn't know for sure. And I feared that my voice would betray my uncertainty, and that my wobbly space of not knowing would break her in a new way.

'My son sleeps like that too,' I said.

Calvin's mother opened her eyes and looked directly at me. What I'd said, the smallness of it, the white lie of it—for that wasn't how Finn slept at all—I'd thought it would bind us. I don't know why I needed or wanted that, but it wasn't the outcome. I'd misjudged the distance between us, which was too huge to be bridged by this trivial note. I could see something bad rising up in Calvin's mother. I'd stepped too far into a space where I wasn't welcome.

'All right,' Calvin's father said.

The three of them—Calvin's mother, father, and sister—stood in unison. It was a coordinated movement that made them seem fastened around the middle with an invisible lasso. It was time for me to leave. I pushed back my chair and I walked down the hallway and out the front door alone.

As I left the neighbourhood, I saw the turnoff for the State Park that was notable because it was where many manatees spent the winter months. I thought I could go for a wander along the boardwalk there, maybe catch a glimpse of a large, smooth, silver back breaking the surface of the clear green water and then slowly floating back down to the sandy bed beneath. Those creatures weren't fit for a nightmare landscape. They were too gentle, too slow moving. While I took a moment to decide what to do—this or home, this or that—I thought of the morning on the prairie when I'd seen the bald eagle. I'd wanted the experience of seeing it to be mine alone, and the lie

I'd told to make that possible, to keep it from Dan, was only a small selfishness. I didn't like it though. Less for the fact of the bird it concealed and more for what it represented, which was that I would always do things I didn't understand. And I would always find it in me to wound. I passed a house similar to Calvin's. A pair of SUVs were parked in that driveway too. A man was out there with a vacuum cleaner, bent over the back seat of one, while a woman stood behind him angrily unrolling a fist of paper towels. Sitting on the front step of the house in a patch of sun was a young teen girl stroking the belly of a fat ginger cat.

That's a family, I thought. I also have a family. My family, they're there and I'm here. They're there and I'm here, but I can go to them anytime I want. Though when I arrived home, they weren't there, and the house was dark.

10.

'The bats are upside down,' Dan said. 'Can you see that, bud?'

'Malayan Flying Fox,' Perry said. He was studying the info card affixed to the enclosure.

'They're hanging from the roof.' Dan spoke brightly into the back of Finn's head.

'Try catching those eyes,' Perry said.

I did as Perry suggested and looked closer at the bat nearest to me. Its eyes were open. They were warm and shimmered with a sweet intelligence. I found myself pulled to the fencing that separated us. I ignored the advice of the signs and hooked my fingers an inch through the wire.

We entered a room where you could view the bats through a wide window. Dan was carrying Finn while I trailed behind with the diaper bag and party supplies, including the cake I'd baked Friday night, buckled into the stroller. The bats in this enclosure weren't doing much. They were hanging from the ceiling in varying states of unwrapping—some hugging themselves, rolled up tight like leathery cigars, others with their wings spread wide in full bat signal pose, some with one wing extended so they appeared twisted, like wet clothes pegged haphazardly on the line.

'Upside-down animals, bud,' Dan said.

These creatures, how did they look to Finn like anything more than woolly wind ornaments? Something for hanging from the ceiling above the porch to twist and whistle in the breeze?

'Animals,' Finn said. That word was a hard one for him. It was a washed out, barely perceptible wreck of a ship.

'I don't think he fully gets it,' I said.

I could see enough of Dan's face to know this was the wrong thing to say.

'Hold on,' Dan said. He flipped Finn upside down, so his feet were kicking in the air. Finn shrieked in a way that suggested he didn't like it.

'Whoa,' Perry said, poking Finn in the belly, 'look at this big bat.'

Dan turned Finn the right way up again. They moved closer to the window of the enclosure, Finn still panting with excitement and a bit of fright. Finn pressed his hands to the glass, spread his fingers into plump starfish.

'That's how the bats are,' Dan said. 'Can you say *bat*?'

'Bat?' Perry said.

'It's an Indian Flying Fox,' I said.

'Bat, buddy?' Dan said. 'Can you?'

Finn wouldn't say it. He wasn't a performer. Maybe he was already figuring out that having some kind of happiness meant not giving yourself over entirely to others, that you always needed to keep something back.

175

The Bat Conservancy was situated in a cluster of low buildings, in a field of grass ringed by Florida pines, forty minutes north of our neighbourhood. To get there we'd driven through what seemed like horse country, judging by the signs and the quality of the fencing around the fields. Our birthday crew consisted of Dan, Finn and me, Perry, Chantelle and Wren, and Chantelle's mother. Now Dan suggested that we needed to find something to eat and to sit down. When we'd first arrived, we'd passed through a crop of food trucks. Chantelle, Wren, and Chantelle's mother were ahead of us. Though we'd entered the long corridor of the bat enclosures together, while we had stalled, they had powered off, Wren at a running pace. Chantelle was different with her mother nearby—her edges sharper, less who I thought she was. I could just make out her red braid as the crowd swallowed her, the closely cropped white hair of her mother beside. They were heading toward the food trucks too.

In the area directly outside the entrance to the bat enclosures there were stalls set up by local conservation groups, many bat-related. Dan and Perry stopped at the table of a non-profit group that built and installed bat houses in domestic yards. Finn stood with them. He reached out and swiped a pamphlet.

As I pulled up beside them with the stroller, Dan turned to me. 'We should do this,' he said.

The man behind the table was wearing a T-shirt printed with bats and Gothic font, and very short cut-offs, his legs dense with tattoos. His hair fell below his shoulders.

'We've got a waitlist right now,' he said. 'Should be good to go mid-summer.'

He directed this information to me as if I was the one who needed convincing.

Dan was nodding away beside me. 'Put us down.'

'Great, let's do it,' the bat guy said. He handed a wooden clipboard to Dan. 'Here.'

The image of two to three hundred bats making their home in our backyard filled me with liquid worry. I could feel it sloshing around up to my eyeballs. 'Stop it,' I said, 'just stop.' I put out my hand before the clipboard could reach Dan.

Dan recoiled.

The bat guy didn't flinch. 'I'll give y'all a minute.'

'Man, I'm so hungry,' Perry said. He bent down to Finn who was clutching multiple pamphlets now. 'Are you hungry, little dude?' He took Finn by the hand and led him away.

What exactly was I afraid of? Did I think the bats wouldn't just live their lives in peace, enjoying their nights out catching insects, and returning before dawn to their snug home at the end of our yard? Did I think they might assume I was inviting them to live in our house? Did I think I would get bitten? Catch something? Or have to experience too many times the feel of those leathery wings brushing, flapping against my skin? Those sweet furry faces, turned-up noses—did I think I might step out of the shower one morning to find them nuzzling against the door, my towel, my pillow?

New Zealand has bats, though I'd never interacted with one in the almost thirty years I'd lived there. In Florida, the bats were plentiful, as much a presence in the evening sky as the feathered heads of the sabal palms. The bat houses on the university campus alone hosted three hundred thousand bats, more than twice the human population of our city—two bats for every person walking the streets of our neighbourhood, one for each shoulder. Maybe it wasn't the bats I was most worried about though. Dan making a decision so impulsively, it wasn't like him. I suspected he was zooming in on this thing out of fright. And that frightened me.

'Do you even know how it feels to have no idea where your family is or if they're ever coming back?' was the first thing I'd said to Dan in the early hours of Thursday morning when he and Finn finally returned home. There had been no note, no message, Dan hadn't picked up my calls, and Perry couldn't tell me where he was, so all I'd been able to do was wait for them to return many hours later in the dark of the night. Without answering me, Dan had gone upstairs and put Finn in his crib. 'Where have you been?' I'd said when he came back down.

'Where do you think we've been?' Dan said.

It was around one in the morning at this point, the two of us standing on opposite sides of the living room. The next thing Dan said was, 'Where are my glasses?'

'I don't know,' I said.

'I had to take my contact lenses out,' he said.

It was only then that I registered that I'd not seen him with glasses on for days and days. He usually moved between glasses and contact lenses, never favouring one version of his face over the other. He also hadn't asked me to inspect his eye since the time in Perry's hallway. I'd thought nothing of it. I hadn't noticed, I'd been so absorbed by my own worries.

'Wait,' I'd said next, forgetting for a minute that I'd had the car, and, more significantly, stuck as I often was on the wrong thing, 'did you drive home without your glasses?'

Dan had looked appalled.

Since the previous Thursday night, when his eye had first started to bother him, Dan had kept his contact lenses in. They seemed to soothe the irritation, which had turned out to be a scratch made by either a flying piece of eggshell or plastic, providing relief but also letting, via the trapped bacteria of lenses that were never perfectly clean, an infection develop. He had thought the itchiness and wateriness, the vague pink hue of that eye, were only leftover irritations from the initial injury. He'd sensed some blurriness, but he'd thought it only tiredness, maybe a smudge on the contact lens. Then, while I was on my road trip, he'd found it increasingly difficult to look at the TV screen. He'd had a bad feeling. So, he'd gone upstairs and looked in the bathroom mirror, seeing for the first time how severely his eyelid was swollen.

Wednesday night's emergency doctor prescribed him antibiotics and told him to return to the eye clinic first thing the following morning. The next day Dan saw an ophthalmologist. She numbed his eye with drops. Then she gently scraped the surface of the pinhead-sized ulcer that was there and clear as day, if you knew to look, to confirm that the source of the infection was bacterial. When Dan returned home after that appointment and filled me in on these details, he spoke slowly and angrily, his right eye still stained yellow from another test, so that he appeared sick, jaundiced, but only on one side.

'I think it's a cool idea,' Dan said now about the bat house.

'Don't you think we should ask our landlord first?' I said.

Dan narrowed his eyes at me.

It had seemed impossible that, first, the contact lenses hadn't made the scratch on Dan's eye feel worse, and next, that this thing had been able to develop without Dan being in excruciating pain. I wanted him to explain it to me by saying, 'I've been in so much pain, Georgie, an exhaustible amount of pain, but I've just been ignoring it. So, the fact that there has been time for this festering to take place, the fact that you didn't see how my eye was constantly tearing up, how pink it had grown, how sensitive I'd become to light, is on me, not you.'

If the ulcer left a scar, Dan's vision could end up being affected. What would that mean for his work? Would it be safe for him to be in the workshop? And what about driving a car, cycling? Even throwing a ball around with his son, would that be harder? They were not life-threatening consequences, but these were the edges of Dan's life and they mattered. I'd watched the reality of these risks sink in for Dan in the last couple of days. It had made it hard for us to come together because it wasn't yet clear where we were going to land. Now, as I watched Dan spin the picture of the bat house in our yard round and round in his mind, I thought that maybe he was doing what I'd been doing—grabbing hold of any new thing that came his way and treating it as a floatation device. Maybe that was a reason to let him have the bat house. Maybe I could learn to live with it.

Dan narrowed his eyes further. He was looking over my shoulder. When I turned around, I saw Gray. He was manning the eastern indigo snake table. They were a conservation group he volunteered for.

'There's your friend,' Dan said. He walked off in the direction of the table behind Perry and Finn.

'Ms Beard,' Gray said, as I approached. He was wearing his usual short-sleeved button-down tucked into his shorts, with socks and loafers.

'Gray,' I said, mirroring his faux formalness. Dan, Perry and Finn had stopped too. I reached down and picked up Finn. 'You remember Dan,' I said. 'And Finn.'

I was amazed to see that Finn extended a hand to Gray, maybe remembering him from that one interaction almost three weeks ago. Gray also extended his hand to Finn, and they shook like two old men over a chessboard in the park, unsmiling, no fanciness.

'How's your morning been?' I said, nodding at the table.

Gray detailed the morning's events, including an intricate retelling of a conversation he'd had with one woman who was convinced that these snakes, not any other kind of snake but this exact rare and endangered breed, were getting into her rabbit hutches and she was here to lodge a complaint. While Gray spoke, I think we did actually forget for a moment when we'd seen each other last, on the burn, just over a week ago. Gray was the one who broke the spell.

'Did you get the message I left on your phone?' he said. 'I called twice because the first time, I didn't believe that was you.'

'No, that's me,' I said.

'You sounded like a harangued spirit.'

'Yes, I got your message,' I said.

In the message, which I'd forgotten about as soon as I'd listened to it, Gray had failed to mention Calvin or the burn and had said only that I should stop by his office at the earliest possible convenience. Now I told him I was sorry, but I'd been busy. He nodded and picked up his canvas satchel, a bag that I'd previously seen propped up on a chair in his office. He removed a burner CD. Nothing had been written on the top of the disc or on the case to indicate what was on there.

'You can play it on your computer laptop,' Gray said.

'What's on it?' I said.

'It might help,' was all Gray said.

It was the kind of thing my father would have done. Back when I still owned CDs, my collection was full of albums my father had given me, sometimes for no reason at all, though more often as a way to say what he couldn't, when he was proud,

181

when he was worried, when he could see I was hurting. All those CDs were still in cardboard boxes in my parents' garage. Whatever was on the CD from Gray, I appreciated it.

'Snuck,' Finn said. This was a new and unfamiliar cluster of letters for him.

'Snuck?' I said.

'Snuck,' Finn said, more forcefully this time.

A couple of tables down a guy in his early twenties, likely a student judging by all his university-branded clothes, was handling a snake with a pattern on its skin that I attributed to a python. This was what Finn was looking at. While I was figuring this out, Gray had walked over to the guy. He came back to us holding the snake, his right hand firmly around a length of its body where its arms would be, if it had arms, his left hand further down, as if he were cradling some elongated infant.

'Here you go,' he said, approaching us from the visitor side of the table.

My most alarming snake encounter to date was on a tubing trip the summer before Finn was born. A group of us rented tubes, caught a dinky train to the top of the river dressed in our swimsuits, and armed with ice-cold PBRs and bottles of Topo Chico, we lazily bobbed our way back down the river under the hot Florida sun. About halfway through our journey I saw a snake fall from a tree into a woman's lap. She was less than twenty feet ahead of us. On realising what it was, the woman threw herself from her tube and began flailing around as if she were drowning, though the water was only four feet deep.

'God help me!' she cried. 'God help me!'

As we floated past, I turned around to try and get a better

look. Two of the woman's companions had rolled out of their own tubes and were struggling to keep their friend calm and buoyed while also wrangling three tubes against the lazy current. The snake had already swum off.

Someone from our group called out to the poor woman: 'There's no need to freak out, it's only a black racer.'

'Go to hell,' one of her friends called back.

I'd seen other snakes in the wild, their quiet and quick disappearances into the grass. I'd scooped snakes from friends' pools. I'd seen them basking on the sidewalk. I'd never touched one though. Today, I didn't have time to feel afraid. Maybe I was spurred on by Finn's genuine interest, that special thing kids have when they're so purely wide open to the world, before they know what could be dangerous. He quickly extended his hand to the tail of the snake, which Gray had done his best to raise to Finn's level. He touched it gently and smiled.

'Hello, sweetie,' I said. I meant it for the snake. 'Take this,' I said to Dan, and handed him Gray's CD to put in the stroller. I wanted to pet the snake too.

'We're gonna order some pizzas,' Dan said. Without waiting for my reply, he took the stroller and went off with Perry.

The snake felt like a precious metal, cool and smooth, but that wasn't exactly right because there was a strange warmth to it too. It wasn't warm to touch—but it emanated it, the warmth of its little snake life, its little snake soul. A shiver zipped up my spine, not of fright, but awe.

'I'm sorry that happened to you,' Gray said. It felt like he'd been waiting for Dan to leave before he said this. 'It shouldn't have happened. You shouldn't have been out there.'

'It's fine,' I said. I was captivated by the snake, as was Finn, and honestly, Gray wanting to discuss this right now, I didn't need it or want it.

'I simply cannot grasp what he was doing still lost out there,' Gray said. 'Someone should've known where he was. Someone must have known.'

'People can probably be good liars when the stakes are high enough,' I said.

'What is higher?' Gray said. He said this first to me, then he lowered his head and he repeated it quietly, as if for the snake. 'What is higher?'

Finn had remained silent this whole time. His fingertips were still lovingly pressed to the skin of the snake. Now, as we turned to leave, he withdrew his hand and I heard him say, quietly, as much for himself as anyone else, the tail end of a two-year-old's internal monologue, but also as clear as anything he'd said up until this point in his life, 'Bye-bye, snuck.'

Hearing that, I felt pride and relief for the simple fact of the clarity of his speech. I also sensed the fresh burn at the beginning of an inevitable loss. Those couple of words were a reminder that—although I understood so little of what my boy said, his shared world still muddy—his internal life already existed in a rich and multi-storied way, and it was all his own and nothing to do with me.

We planted ourselves in the sectioned-off part of the Fair where local breweries had set up stalls. You couldn't buy the beer because the Bat Conservancy didn't have a liquor licence, but you could pay a special entrance fee that allowed you to 'free taste test' as many beers as you wanted. I was the sober driver. I didn't say a word about Dan drinking on antibiotics. We managed to co-opt two tables, three bar stools, and a few hay bales. Chantelle was also the sober driver for her party, and her mother, Dan, and Perry were already investigating another round. Finn and Wren were both standing beside a hay bale, gnawing and sucking their pizza slices.

'How's Dan?' Chantelle said.

I explained that we were waiting to see how the eye healed, fought off the infection. How Dan had the drops and the pills and another appointment in a week.

'Dan said the ophthalmologist was non-judgmental,' I said. 'It made me think that maybe this was something she saw a lot—people in pain ignoring that pain because it didn't feel as pressing or as painful as the other things in their lives.'

Chantelle nodded as if she understood completely. I'd still not told her everything about what had happened in the last week. I'd told her some. She got it though. The specifics of it all maybe not mattering so much in the end. We stood quietly for a moment and watched our sons eat their pizza.

'I had an ex who was blind in one eye,' she said, finally. 'He had a fake ceramic eye he could remove. His real eye was still there but dead. The fake eye was a tiny shield he wore in front of the dead eye. I picked it up once by accident, the fake eye. It was sitting on the bedside table, upside down on a saucer. What's this? I thought, and I picked it up and turned it over.'

'What happened?' I said.

'It scared the bejeezus out of me is what happened,' she said. 'Those things are realistic. My brain truly thought I was holding his eye in the palm of my hand.'

Chantelle held out her hand while she said this, and we both looked at it, her palm facing the wide, grey sky. I tried to imagine Dan's eye resting there. The iris would be dark blue cut with rivers of turquoise. Though I feared that if the eye was outside of his head and not with the rest of his face, I wouldn't recognise it, wouldn't know it was his. There was an episode from a game show in my childhood where a woman won a thousand dollars because she could pick out one of her dairy cows from a line-up of cows while blindfolded, knowing her cow using only her hands, by touch. As a child I'd thought this extraordinary. Now the memory of it filled me with panic, as if my inability to accurately conjure this horrible image—Dan's detached eye sitting in the palm of my friend's hand—was a sign that we were done.

'Don't look now,' Chantelle said, closing her hand into a fist.

I turned around and saw Loren and Alexander and a woman I assumed was Alexander's other mother walking towards us. They were holding hands in a line and dressed in matching Bat Conservancy caps. I'd completely forgotten that I'd invited them. I waved, and watched as Loren waved back with a grimace. As she got closer, I saw that she was wearing full makeup, as if she was stopping by here on her way out to dinner and a show.

'You came,' I said, when they were close enough to hear.

'We did,' she said, 'I hope that's okay.'

I heard Chantelle grunting with disapproval beside me.

'Love your hats,' I said.

'Those hats are cool,' Dan said.

Chantelle's mother, Dan and Perry had returned armed with a tray of a dozen very small glasses of beer.

'I wouldn't mind one of those hats,' Perry said.

Dan and Perry exchanged a nod. They were already many samples in, and though I didn't think of Dan as being a lightweight drinker, he seemed much wobblier than I would have expected. Maybe it was the antibiotics. He had a cheeriness that was impossible to categorise as either real or put on.

We settled into each other's company. Loren, with her wife Justine next to her, was light, funny, right at home in our party. Chantelle quickly thawed to her, more concerned by the presence of her mother, who was second guessing everything Chantelle said and did for Wren, clearly just wanting to be in on it, but not giving Chantelle her space or her due. Dan, Perry and Justine formed a huddle and spent a lot of time talking about cycling trails and breweries. If I hadn't been such a giant ball of worry, I would have been able to think what I would think at a time in the future when I was with these friends, which was how one of the truest pleasures of being alive and human was shooting the shit with good people.

Dan reached into the basket of the stroller and brought out Finn's birthday cake. It was meant to be a bat. I'd baked in a daze. I'd forgotten to grease the cake tins or use baking paper and the cakes had come out with jagged edges and one with a gaping hole in the middle. There was a lot of frosting glue hidden below the top layer of decorative frosting.

'Where're the candles?' Dan said.

I felt my eyes grow wide. 'Oh god,' I said. 'I didn't even think.'

'No kidding,' Dan said.

The coldness of his tone when he said this was half-hearted. It wasn't mixed with any warmth, but had its back against nothing—ambivalence. From where I was standing, I couldn't see the shape and ridge of his ulcer, but it was there, and it was what filled him up. Whatever Dan's concerns about us, his hatred for Jason, maybe his hatred for me, there wasn't room for these things in his person right now. Except for this—a weak cold look in my direction.

'The candles don't matter,' Perry said. 'Don't need 'em.'

'Probably not safe near all this hay anyway,' Loren said.

'Yeah, it's not a big deal,' I said.

Then I watched Dan's coldness morph in front of my eyes. He looked at me now with something closer to rage. He started raking his top teeth across his bottom lip. He was trying to keep it all in, not wanting to do this here. I don't know what I was doing, probably looking at him in this way too, though I was less angry and more on fire with uncertainty. Everything around us became a distant ringing in my ears, the comments from our friends swirling: we'll just sing Happy Birthday, look let's cut the cake, Finn, you want cake, Wren, Xander, who else, who wants more beer, I'll join you, us too, I'm gonna go pee. Eventually it was me and Dan alone, and the kids—Finn, Alexander, and Wren—still standing around their bales, each of them gripping their slice of cake for dear life.

'I thought you were having fun,' I said to Dan. It was all I could think to say.

'I wouldn't say that,' he said.

Just then, a scowling pregnant woman, with a man and two kids, stalked past us. I was reminded of a woman I'd met in the corridor on the way to the one birthing class Dan and I had attended. That woman had been pregnant with her fourth child, and she was enraged about it. She was attending the class alone. That day, I sat as far away from her as possible, not wanting to be anywhere near those vibes. I've since thought of her and wondered how she was doing, if things turned out okay.

'I think you should say what you want to say,' I said to Dan.

'You never even said sorry,' he said.

I hadn't thought once about Jason the whole morning. He'd twisted his way into my thoughts the night before when I was alone in the kitchen baking Finn's cake. I'd let myself test the waters, once again playing out the events inside the library room, as I'd done several times since Wednesday afternoon. What I wanted to know was—if I arrived on his doorstep and knocked on his front door, would he let me in? I couldn't get a grip on the shape or weight of what might happen after, so the best I could do for now was wonder whether I would be granted entry. Would I enter though? That I also didn't know. Now, as I considered what Dan had said, Jason felt very far away, as if the whole thing had happened to someone else. My life, it was all right here: an ugly bat cake cut poorly onto paper plates, my kid and his friends, hay bales, tiny beer samples, my husband waiting, breathing deeply, still violently raking his teeth across his lip, the sky a warm grey blanket above us.

'Where did you put the CD?' I said to Dan. I suddenly thought that since handing it over to him, I hadn't seen it. 'The one Gray gave me.'

'That's what you want to know right now?' Dan said.

I knew then that he'd thrown the CD away. That it was lying in a trash can somewhere in our vicinity. For Dan, it wasn't about Gray, but about territory. He couldn't see Gray's kindness, because for too long now what he regarded as his territory had been run wild with all kinds of people and things. So this was the patch on which he'd chosen to stake out his claim, and though I wanted to know what was on the CD, I wouldn't go looking.

'It doesn't matter,' I said.

'You're right it doesn't matter,' Dan said.

Finn looked up at us then. He was still fiercely clutching the remains of his birthday cake. The frosting was spread across the entire bottom half of his face. His broken teeth shone through.

189

For the first time, I noticed how his eyes were the exact shade between my pale blues and Dan's dark blues. Our eyeballs would form a satisfyingly precise colour gradient chart.

'No?' Dan said, returning to the earlier part of our conversation. 'You never even apologised, Georgie.'

'I just,' I said, 'I don't know that I am sorry.'

'Morning, Finn,' Finn said. 'Morning, Finn.'

He didn't want to go down for his nap. He believed that if he said this, the thing Dan and I said to him in the mornings when he woke, it would speed up or reverse time in such a way that he could be getting out of bed rather than into it. It was nearly two hours later than his usual nap time and he was delirious with tired and too much sugar. On the drive home from the Bat Conservancy, Dan had sat in the back seat to entrance him into staying awake, so he could go to sleep in his bed. 'Morning Finn morning Finn,' he garbled all the way up the stairs. He flapped his arms and arched his back while I wrestled him into his crib, read him a single story, then light out, white-noise machine on. He was asleep before I left the room. Flat on his back, arms to his side, knees out, the soles of his feet neatly pressed together, so from above he looked like a frog dreamily gliding on the surface of a pond.

Back downstairs I found Dan sitting at the kitchen table with a fresh beer open in front of him. He was looking out the glass sliding doors into our yard, transfixed.

I'd waited for him to react to my non-apology. Instead, he'd acquiesced. I'd thought I'd seen the shadow of a shrug as he'd turned away from me, shaded his eyes from the glare of the sun with his hand, and said, 'I'm gonna find one of those hats.'

'What's up with that?' I said now, meaning the beer.

He didn't respond. I'd thought that once we were safe inside the walls of our home he might come out with it, that we might return to the scene. He was wearing the cap he'd bought. It was peach-coloured, the bat illustration and text stitched on the front in blue.

'Fair enough,' I said.

I went to the kitchen, switched on the kettle and stared out the window, so Dan and I were looking at the same thing.

'There's a raccoon out there,' I said.

'I'm watching it,' Dan said. 'It looks unwell.'

I walked to the sliding door. The raccoon standing in the yard was noticeably skinny. There was nothing else outwardly wrong-looking about it, no wounds or foaming at the mouth, only that it was out in the middle of the day and that it seemed, for want of a better word, confused.

'You think?' I said.

'It's unwell,' Dan said, definitively.

'We should call Animal Control.'

'Hmm,' Dan said. He slowly lifted his can of beer to his mouth and took a swig. He didn't take his eyes off the creature in our yard.

'Where's my phone?' I said, scanning the room.

When I returned, Dan was no longer sitting at the table. While I was searching for the Animal Control number I saw him appear from around the side of the house clutching a spade. I walked to the sliding door, opened it. I couldn't see the raccoon anywhere.

'What're you doing?' I said.

'Do you want to have a sick raccoon living in our yard?'

'I think it came from that bush,' I said.

'I know,' Dan growled.

191

He was striding towards the row of shrubs lined up against the back fence. I saw him brush at the bushes with the spade. I wondered if he expected me to help. Though I suspected the animal had moved on, I didn't like the thought of it taking up residence so close to our living space, especially if it was sick.

'It's not distemper season,' Dan said.

'How do you know that?' I said.

'I know things too,' he said.

'It was moving oddly,' I said. 'With "swagger" even.'

'I wouldn't use that word,' Dan said.

'It seemed confident,' I said.

Dan swished the spade across the surface of some other bushes. 'There's nothing here,' he said, swiping at a healthy agave plant, no hiding place for a raccoon. 'Where'd it go?'

He stood and looked around our yard. It seemed to me that whatever had possessed him inside the house and had made him stride out here with his spade swinging, was waning.

'You can't leave it out here,' I said.

'If I can't find it,' Dan said, 'there's not much I can do about it, is there?'

He was standing beside me now. He rested the spade on his shoulder as if he were a Viking taking a drinks break in the middle of a battle. I thought of Calvin's mother, father, and sister, how I'd seen them last—standing together around their kitchen table as if they were fused together. I wondered if Dan felt this way about me, and if he did was it a good feeling for him, being part of a united front, or did he feel stuck? That, I think, was a lot of it. I was worried he felt stuck with me, as I did with him.

From where I was standing, I could see how the old heather-grey T-shirt he was wearing was visibly disintegrating around the neck. Also against his neck was the shine of the gold chain that held his wedding band, which he'd worn like this since he'd started working in the workshop. I'd not worn my ring since I was pregnant with Finn.

The night Dan and I met, at that party above the car repair shop, he'd had his back to the wall, watching the band while hunched over and nodding with a half-enthusiasm to a much shorter woman. As I observed him, he'd looked up and towards where I stood in the crowd maybe ten yards away. His face unchanged, he'd then turned back to the woman. A moment later though, he looked up again, unmistakably at me, and for what felt like the longest time neither of us looked away. Now I noticed how, though his eyes were shaded by the peak of his cap, he scrunched up the right side of his face. Behind his glasses his damaged eye was still sensitive and paining him. I kept forgetting about his eye and having to remember the whole thing all over again. There was something wrong with me. Why was it so easy for me to forget about Dan? Had I always been like this?

Suddenly a string of obscenities punctured the air above us. A man was yelling from high up, the insults travelling over our heads. I guessed it was from one of the nearby two-storey houses being tented for termites, that maybe they were ready to take down the scaffolding. I'd never previously lived in a place where so much energy was expended on keeping undesirable creatures out of one's yard, one's home, one's heart.

'Termites,' I said to Dan, my tone suggesting what I believed, which was that I was an expert on trespassers.

'Us next.'

'What do you mean?' I said.

'Landlord called last night when you were out on your walk.

We gotta get out first thing tomorrow.'

Just that morning I'd seen that a banana spider as big as my hand had taken up residence on our porch. In New Zealand, I'd killed spiders brutally and with no guilt. But the impressive long-legged creature I'd almost face-planted into as I'd rushed out with all the things for Finn's party, and which I saw again in the afternoon when I returned from the Bat Conservancy with him in my arms, it wouldn't survive the tenting if left alone. I made a mental note to rehome it before we moved out, and in the shadow of that thought I saw something of who I was becoming.

'Thanks for telling me?' I said to Dan.

'She's booked us a room at her B&B.' Dan turned and briefly looked down at me. 'She emailed a list of stuff we have to do in preparation.'

Before he looked back up, he adjusted his cap and sniffed. I glimpsed the sharp point of his widow's peak, and it all came at me in a rush. All the missed opportunities, wrong turns, my parts, his parts, and it seemed to me like we'd been standing here for a long time, in this exact spot, side by side, trying to find something that we weren't sure was even there, trying to find it so we could what, scare it away, trap it, destroy it? It also felt like this could go on forever, looking for this raccoon that was or wasn't sick, this horrible state of our relationship. We could stand like this for another fifty years and die like this. I feared Dan was already planning his escape. I knew I wouldn't be able to leave him though. Whenever I tried to picture it, fleeing, I couldn't. I wasn't an outlaw. I'm not too cool to admit that.

I never told anyone how much I hated and feared swimming in the seas of my childhood because I didn't want to seem like a wimp. So, I learned to find a joy in the pain of it as well as the pride of being the first one to emerge from the surf onto the wet black sand, my blood thumping through me, my eyes raw from the salt, the muscles in my legs and arms quickly softening. I wouldn't sit down right away though. It felt too good to be upright in myself with the sea at my back, momentarily conquered. The man who was attacked by a tiger shark while swimming in those same rough waters, he'd had a wife and two teenaged kids. He'd been the owner of a substantial plant nursery. All they'd been able to rescue of him after the shark had had its way was a leg, an arm, a flap of digestive organs. There was always that possibility. I still needed him, Dan. I'd been looking for a fresh happiness to escape from the familiar unhappiness of my marriage. The new happiness wouldn't last, I knew that, so what it came down to was really a trade of unhappinesses. That was a different thing. I'd been thinking about it all wrong. Though how much unhappiness was the right amount?

This here, what Dan and I were doing now, was one way for us to be together. Maybe we just needed to find a different way. Was this the real bridge to what came after, and where all the answers really lay?

'I'd rather just fuck you, you know,' I said.

'Maybe you should prove it,' Dan said.

I felt a rupture in my chest.

That's when the raccoon made its reappearance. Like an aged actor rolling on to the stage for a dramatic cameo, it crawled slowly and regally out of the bush where I'd seen it earlier, and stumbled towards us, its back legs clearly dragging now. Dan was right, there was something wrong with it.

'Oh shit,' I said. I sounded both excited and scared. I was

trying to hold these three things in my mind: what I'd said to Dan, Dan's response, the raccoon.

'Whoa,' Dan said, 'there you are.'

The raccoon was suddenly just several yards away. It looked up and directly at me, and as we held each other's gaze, it slowly and viciously licked its lips. I felt puny, reduced.

'Is it going to pounce?' I said.

There was an undeniable coldness in the raccoon's eyes. I was unable to move. Dan slowly lowered the spade till it was extended between us and the animal. If you'd asked me to say what I hoped Dan would do next, I would have said something along the lines of: He raised the spade and pummelled that raccoon and its diseased brain to smithereens, before turning to me, raccoon spray on the front of his T-shirt, a couple of drips of something caught up in the stubble of his chin, and saying, 'There.'

'Wow,' I would say.

'No worries,' he would say.

'No worries?' I would say.

'Yeah,' Dan would say. He would be smiling. He would wipe his arm across his face.

'Your mouth,' I would say, 'did it go in your mouth?'

'A bit,' he would say.

Then we would both start laughing because Dan would make me want to laugh. He would suddenly appear so light, as if something had been exorcised from him. From us. In the fantasy version of this interaction, it would feel like one of the animal pelts between us had been lifted away. Then we would go into our house and, now wholly different people, we would fuck our relationship back into existence.

In reality, this kind of animal interaction was not standard

196

practice for a boy who grew up on Auckland's North Shore. I don't think they even had possums over there in his childhood neighbourhood of early-Nineties era small-scaled McMansions. Though Dan once told me a story of how when he was a kid he made a possum trap out of a used onion sack. He threaded a length of rope around the opening of the large woven bag, tied the rope to a sturdy branch of a pōhutukawa in his yard, and placed an apple inside. The idea was that the possum would be enticed by the apple, climb into the sack, after which its weight would pull the opening shut. This part of his design worked. What Dan hadn't foreseen was how easy it would be for the possum to claw its way out of the bottom of the loosely woven material.

What actually happened with the raccoon was that the animal, maybe feeling cornered, though it had plenty of room to turn and run, and despite its back legs not being in full working order, leapt at Dan with a shrill growl, teeth bared. In response to this Dan swung the spade up, not with any kind of violence, but as a frightened reflex. This had the odd result of sending the raccoon flying, straight up at first, and then straight down, so the animal ended up on the grass half standing, half on its side. While it was disoriented, Dan and I turned and ran inside our house and locked the door.

'I'll call Animal Control,' Dan said.

While Dan looked for a number, we both remained at the sliding door. The raccoon looked smaller and less threatening from that distance. As well, when we'd dashed inside I'd briefly looked across to our neighbour's apartment, and I'd seen the woman who lived there standing in her living room watching us. The knowledge of this filled me with unease.

'That wasn't good,' Dan said.

'That's one way to put it,' I said.

'Sometimes I forget where we are,' he said. 'That we live here and not there.'

'Not me,' I said. 'I never do.'

We had an hour before the guy from Animal Control was due to arrive. We wouldn't go upstairs. That moment had passed. Instead, we sat side by side on the couch, not speaking. Dan had already got up a few times to peer into the yard and check on the raccoon, which was sitting exactly where we'd left it. Now he sank back into the couch, close to me this time.

'You don't own being angry,' he said.

I could feel him looking at the profile of me, down my forehead, the bridge of my nose, my chin, over my breasts, belly, lap, legs, to my feet where they rested on the coffee table. We needed to wake Finn, so his late nap didn't eat too far into his night sleep. I was trying not to think about that though, the worries of the day, like every day, Finn and his sleeping and eating and speaking and whether the rough skin on his thighs was more or less rough than the day before—it had felt not good as I'd wrestled him into his crib. I was trying to push all that away, to be there with Dan and to move through whatever this was to its end. It felt within reach.

'I don't know what you mean by that,' I said.

'Yeah, you do,' Dan said.

'I think,' I said, searching, 'I'm just too porous.'

'That's how you see yourself?' It was clear from his tone that he didn't think of me this way at all.

I turned in my seat enough that we were facing. Dan's eyes were wide open. Behind the lens of his glasses I could see the ulcer on his right eye. It was a small grey point, like a crescent from the tiniest of eggshells. There were so many ways to hurt a person, so many ways to mess up, to do it wrong. I reached for Dan. I pressed the palm of my hand to his chest. I could feel his heart beating. Slowly, and then quickening.

When I eventually spoke, I did so with the absurd and quivering gravity of someone who had built up this moment in their head, believing it the key to unlocking something poignant and a way forward.

'What did you see?' I said.

'What did I see?' Dan said.

'What did you see.'

'When?'

I don't know why I thought he would know what I was talking about. He didn't have access to my thoughts. He couldn't read my mind, as I couldn't read his mind. He was one person. I was another, entirely different person.

'It doesn't matter,' I said, unable to disguise the disappointment in my voice. I moved to stand up. 'I gotta wake Finn.'

Now it was Dan's turn to reach for me. He placed his hand on my back. The warmth and pressure of that tiny gesture, it stirred something in me.

'Hey,' he said, 'hey.'

'Yes?' I said.

'Let him sleep another five.'

'A short five,' I said.

I reluctantly leaned back into our couch. I was never not anxious about Finn's routine. It was just one thread of the boy who would pull Dan and I through the rest of our lives. Whether we remained together or not, Finn would always be the direction in which we were headed.

My last meal before becoming a parent was from the Wendy's in the hospital foodcourt. There was just enough time between learning that I urgently needed to be induced and being admitted for me to eat—enough calories, I remember thinking, to sustain me across the wide desert of labour. When I was done, Dan and I rode the elevator back up to the maternity ward. Dan took a photo. In it I am smiling all-teeth like a woman about to walk on stage to receive an award. The elevator walls behind me are decorated with silhouettes of Florida wildlife: manatees, alligators, butterflies, turtles, long-beaked and long-legged water birds. The walls are a cheap, pale wood veneer and the silhouettes a range of greys. Finn wouldn't be born till late the following night, but here we were: the two of us riding our way to becoming three of us. When I examine this photo now, I can see that beneath my grin is a reasonable mix of nervous and tired. Though I'm also overflowing with dumb optimism, and that makes me think: Who even is that woman? And: What a little fool.

Now Dan bent his knee and extended his leg over the coffee table in a stretch.

'Everyone I know is unhappy,' I said.

'Yes,' Dan said, in a tone that suggested this wasn't news to him.

It was my turn to glance over his body. He was still as lean as the evening I'd met him, with only a slight softening at the edges. I believed there wasn't an inch of his body I didn't know. I could sense him watching me. I thought maybe I would be able to pick out his eyeballs in a line-up. The damaged one and the good one.

Dan extended both legs then. He lifted his arms above his head and pressed his palms back against the wall. Seeing him

200

like that made me want to stretch too. I raised my arms over my head in the same way. Though I couldn't reach the wall, I extended as far as I could. I heard a joint crack. I couldn't tell you which one of us that sound came from.

11.

'Want some?' Gray said. He was holding out a pack of gum.

I wasn't a gum chewer. Out there in the forest, though, it felt like the right thing to do, to say yes, and so I always said yes.

Ed was holding out a drip torch. 'Georgie, this one's yours.'

'Everyone watered?' Fran said.

I'd consumed a full two pints before getting out of the car. I had another bottle secured to the back of the bike. It was impossible to drink too much water. I never needed to pee. Even with my bladder, it wasn't a problem.

'Just a small patch today,' Gray said. He was standing with his arms crossed against his chest, looking into the trees.

The day before my second prescribed burn Gray made it clear to me that there was no shame in never returning to the forest. I think he was confused as to why I wanted to go back. 'I'll be there,' was all I said. When Dan asked why I wanted to go back, I told him the story about jumping from the rocks as a kid, how I'd hated it, how I'd done it anyway. He already knew the story, but still he said that he understood. Dan and me. The big happinesses and unhappinesses were bookends only to the act of keeping on, and keeping on together. It wasn't rocket science, and yet this realisation made me feel like I'd arrived somewhere.

Today Fran and I were on drip torches while Gray worked behind us with his rake. Ed would be coming up the rear on the bike. I wasn't allowed to drive the bike yet, though I'd set my heart on it, the honour of riding with the equipment, and keeping watch.

'Whoa,' Ed called over the whip and crackle of the fire and the low rev of the bike's engine. 'Step back, Georgie, step back.'

I hadn't been watching where I was walking. I was getting too close to the fire. Fran turned and looked at me. I could sense how she narrowed her eyes at me from behind her sunglasses. She'd not yet forgiven me for what she'd had to see too. Though it wasn't my fault, there was no one else for her to blame. I took it as best as I could. In some ways, it was a privilege to be the bearer of all that hurt, to be the person whose job it was, throw after throw, to catch the bad feelings and then lob them away, to lighten the load.

'Sorry,' I said. 'I wasn't looking.'

Fran turned back to her work. Ed continued on ahead.

Calvin hadn't gone anywhere, would never leave entirely. Even if, like Loren said, one day I could get over it, he had already settled into my consciousness in a different way. He had become less of an intruder and more like a roommate. I would get used to him being there. I would get used to the moments when it all came rushing back. I would learn to think of what I'd seen, what I'd brushed up against, not as a piece of some bigger puzzle that was wide and opaque and needed to be fitted together with difficulty, but rather as a simple reminder that life could so easily go wrong, that there were so many ways for it to do so, so you should take what you can get.

I heard Fran curse. 'Here it comes,' she said.

The smoke. It swelled. The wind had shifted. In an instant I couldn't see three yards in front of my face. There was no way to know if I was still walking in the right direction, toeing the fire line, veering too close, or too far.

'Georgie,' Gray said. He was suddenly standing to my left. 'You all right?'

'I think so,' I said.

The smoke stung my eyes, but that was the smallest way to think of it. It swirled and it hurt but it was something more than that too. I tried to really look at it. It wasn't a monotone sheet, but a denser thing of many colours and with its own shape. I felt I could reach out my hand, briefly hold it, and then feel it pour through my fingers, as if it were alive.

What I hadn't realised for the longest while was that what I wanted could change. I was allowed to want different things at different times. I was also allowed to be unsure.

I continued moving forward with caution. One step at a time. I heard Ed calling out from the bike. I heard Gray, who had already fallen back into the wall of smoke behind me, calling back. Fran called out now too. The intensity of working towards this singular goal, our voices long lengths of string connecting us, binding our team, was a kind of sport.

Though the truth of it was that we'd arrived, we'd stomped all over it, and now this, it was everything we could do to try and make a bit better what we had wrecked.

'Too much. Too much.'